Back Home With Evangeline

Michele Doucette

Back Home With Evangeline

Copyright © 2011 by Michele Doucette, St. Clair Publications

All rights reserved. No part of this publication may be reproduced or transmitted in any form or by any means, electronic or mechanical, including photocopying, recording, or by any information storage and retrieval system, without written permission from the author.

This is a work of fiction. Names, characters, businesses, places, events and incidents are either the products of the author's imagination or have been used in a fictitious manner. Any resemblance to actual persons, living or dead, or actual events is purely coincidental.

ISBN 978-1-935786-02-3

Printed in the United States of America by

St. Clair Publications

PO Box 726

McMinnville, TN 37111-0726

http://stclairpublications.com/

In considering the consequences that are inconsequential, all that is improbable then becomes probable.
Albert Stewart

......when you have eliminated the impossible, whatever remains, however improbable, must be the truth.
Sir Arthur Conan Doyle (words as spoken by Sherlock Holmes), The Sign of Four, 1890.

Table of Contents

Reviews

PRAISE FOR THE PREQUEL …

A Travel in Time to Grand Pré is unlike anything I've ever read. Not just a novel, it is a unique exploration of the past, with genealogy, Biblical archaeology, metaphysics, the French Acadian people and modern DNA findings.

A unique, fascinating plunge into history, this author has forced me to remember, and to dwell upon, her words often.

Glenda A. Bixler, Independent Professional Book Reviewer
http://gabixlerreviews-bookreadersheaven.blogspot.com/

Michele Doucette has spun a fascinating tale of the eighteenth century Acadians, with characters that are realistic and historical places that are in-depth as well as vivid.

Readers will be both educated and entertained as they travel with Madeleine on this most interesting journey of self discovery.

I was very impressed with the *Message for the 21st Century* chapter at the end of the book, making this a wonderful conclusion to a thought-provoking novel.

Shirley Roe, Allbooks Review International http://www.allbooksreviewint.com/

This novel reads like a travel journal, with historical research evident on each page.

Complete with genealogy charts and inspirational quotes, readers will gain great perspective, not only on the history of the French Acadian people, but also the Knights Templar and the Merovingians, with the spiritual undertones appealing to fans of mystical fiction.

Rebecca Cochran, Historical Novel Society Reviewer http://www.historicalnovelsociety.org/

Back Home With Evangeline

Madeleine Sinclair has always been fascinated with all things Acadian. Her best childhood memories were spent with her grandparents in Nova Scotia. They had honeymooned at Grand Pré and Madeleine knew that someday she'd visit there herself.

Destiny calls and one day Madeleine makes the trip. Overwhelmed by the whole experience, she finds herself fainting in front of the statue of Evangeline. When she awakes, she immediately senses that something is different. Yes, she was in Grand Pré, but the year was now 1754. Madeleine was there to learn the secret of her family heritage in order to walk into her place in history.

A Travel in Time to Grand Pré beautifully meshes historical fact and fiction into Madeleine's story. The details this author provides brings the past (and possibilities) to life and meaningfully connects them to the present day; not just names, dates and detailed genealogies, but also the richness of the Acadian culture and its people. I feel like I've shared a moment or two with these people.

Tami Brady, TCM Reviews http://www.tcm-ca.com/

I feel like I have just been on a wild ride of discovery; not only were there tantalizing historical facts that gave flesh to the saga of the plight of the Acadians and the rich history of this area, but the wealth of metaphysical information was, at times, overwhelming.

This book has affected me in a way that is hard to explain. Suffice it to say that as one who has recently made it a priority in their life to seek The Answer, The Truth, The Explanation of Who We Are and Why We Are Here, I was finding all kinds of answers and leads to the next potential discovery.

In addition to the history of the Acadians, Madeleine and Michel felt like actual living characters to me. I enjoyed the information that, no doubt, includes this author's own family history.

Mariel Barney Hunkeler, Ghost PRO (Paranormal Research Organization)

PRAISE FOR THE SEQUEL …

Michele Doucette is one of those rare authors who has the ability to capture the twinkle of light that plays upon deep waters.

By continuing to embrace her inner feminine wisdom, she has written a uniquely-fitting sequel to *A Travel in Time to Grand Pré,* with both stories embracing the love that whispers during warm summer nights across Acadian fields.

While *Back Home with Evangeline* takes us back to a time of romance and chivalry, desperation and despair, it captures the triumph of the heart; that one true moment when anything is possible!

William F. Mann, author of *The Knights Templar in the New World: How Henry Sinclair Brought the Grail to Acadia* and *The Templar Meridians: The Secret Mapping of the New World.*

Back Home with Evangeline is a fascinating book that involves time travel from the past (Acadie) to present-day Nova Scotia. Linking characters with actual history, and culminating in a spiritual message which is beautiful, I applaud the well-documented research of this author, one that has been merged together with the metaphysical, for readers who delight in both genres.

Bettye Johnson, author of *Secrets of the Magdalene Scrolls* (Book I) and *Mary Magdalene, Her Legacy* (Book II)

All possibilities exist, therefore magic exists; hence the story of Madeleine and Michel. If we could remember past lives, amazing truths would come to light; stuff that would make magic a reality. This is such a book, with incredible life lessons that are there for the taking!

Jean-Guy Poirier, Canada

I very much liked the way fact and fiction were blended together; there was no way to truly know when fact gave way to fiction. I also loved the way the characters moved through time, aware of their missions, finding the chapter where Madeleine and Michel unwrapped the treasures, brought forward from the past, to be an intensely moving one. I loved the way you had the characters sharing their metaphysical knowledge with one another (and with us). That was when I really had to slow down and meditate a bit on what had been read.

This novel contains so much information; a fact that I loved because there was not a single moment when my mind was not intrigued and challenged.

When characters seem so real and tangible it might be because ... they could be.

Mariel Barney Hunkeler, Ghost PRO (Paranormal Research Organization)

In this second book, twin souls, Madeleine and Michel, find themselves transported from 1775 to 2005, back to the Grand Pré of the twenty first century. Married in 1775, they bring valuable writings and artifacts with them to be used for the enlightenment of humanity.

With many distinct threads that include the Acadians, Cathars, Knights Templar and the Holy Grail (the sacred bloodline of Yeshua (Jesus) carried down through the early Frankish Kings), skillfully woven together to create a rich tapestry, as well as meticulously researched historical events that frame the novel, the design of this marvelous work reaches its completion in several key messages from Yeshua, thereby outlining his true Gnostic teachings.

Of particular interest to me was the inclusion of Lawrence's Order of Dispersion, as noted in the prologue; an action that led to the Acadian deportment from Nova Scotia in 1775.

Mary Mageau, award-winning composer and author of *Preparing for Ascension* (ebook) and *Our Chakra System: A Portal to Inter-dimensional Consciousness* (ebook)

Author's Note

As always, continued thanks to Shaun George of New Minas, Nova Scotia, for granting me the distinct privilege of using several of his photographs, both front and back cover, as the visual representatives of the Gaspereau area of Nova Scotia; likewise for his photograph of the Gaspereau River, located on the first page (inside cover) of the book. I hope that many of you will take the time to view his online Flickr photos at http://www.flickr.com/photos/23641763@N08/

I wish to thank Kent Hesselbein for the absolutely stunning book cover design. In his visionary genius, he is *always* able to capture the essence of my feelings.

I also wish to extend my heartfelt thanks to Jean Doris LeBlanc, genealogical archivist at *Les Trois Pignons* in Chéticamp, Cape Breton, Nova Scotia, for her time and effort; friend as well as editor, she took the time to offer necessary constructive criticism.

Thanks must also be conveyed to author William F. Mann for entertaining my Templar related questions.

Forever beholden to my maternal grandmother, Catherine (Kay) Breau, who inspired me with both an abiding love for my French Acadian heritage as well as a need to know more, mere words cannot adequate express the depth of my feelings. Having honeymooned there in September 1930, it is her gentle figure that graces the next page of this book.

As my husband is so fond of saying … *within reach is what is attainable*; *beyond reach is what is imaginable*.

May you, too, reach for the imaginable by listening to your heart and remaining true to what you know to be *your* truth.

With over 6.5 billion people sharing this planet, there are actually 6.5 billion realities, viewpoints, truths, opinions and ways of expressing.

You simply have to recognize that which belongs to you, for you, alone, must walk your path.

Mary Catherine (Breau) Feeley

Honeymoon at Grand Pré, September 1930

Dedication

To my hale and hearty French Acadian ancestors who left Old France to travel to the New World, tilling the soil of Acadie, willing to embrace a new life for themselves and their families.

To these same ancestors, a forsaken people living in lands fought over by both British and French counterparts, totally unprepared for the desolate event of 1755 with some families being forever separated; they still managed to survive, starting anew like the rising Phoenix.

To these same ancestors, an abandoned people, totally unprepared for the outcome of the Deportation, many were forced to give their lives to the stormy waves of the Atlantic Ocean, based on the deplorable condition of the ships.

With some making it to Old France, there were many who were immediately imprisoned upon reaching a foreign country, caught up in a battle that was not of their making.

To Michael Jackson, the *King of Pop*; clearly, music was his love, his outlet, one that he shared with the world. In many ways, he was an icon ahead of his time.

Throughout the writing of this book, I was continuously encouraged by my husband's unwavering belief in my ability to pen words to paper. After twenty-six years of dedication to each other, he remains my own special hero.

I trust that my children, Alyssa and Niall, will be proud of this written effort that their mother has made. In addition, I know that they, too, will locate their artistic passions so as to enjoy their own adventures in this game we call life.

Special Message

My name is Sophia Sinclair LeBlanc. For those of you who know my parents, Madeleine Sinclair and Michel dit Sophie LeBlanc, theirs was a most surreal love story.

Having been able to settle on thirty acres of south facing, cleared farmland in Upper Granville, situated on the majestic Annapolis River, located west of Bridgetown, was a dream come true for my parents. In truth, it was an idyllic setting to have been raised.

Ours has been a magical life, to be sure. As my mother was so fond of saying, whether you choose to believe or not, the ancients had a name for us, the people living out these days in the twenty-first century.

Measurements of time, some dating back 18,000 years, foresaw the birth of a powerful generation.

Consequently, all who read this book are living during the 'no time' that was long ago prophesied by the ancients; the time of interface between worlds.

I shall do my best to continue the story that my mother so lovingly began. In doing so, I wish to leave you with her words.

Embrace your inner wisdom.

Embrace the knowingness that these ancient texts spoke of this time when writing the words ... you who walk between the worlds ... for we are the very ones who are now standing on the precipice to a brand new world.

Nova Scotia's British Governor, Charles Lawrence, wrote these words, dated August 11, 1755 … "clear the whole country of bad subjects ... and disperse them among ... the colonies upon the continent of America. Collect them up by any means. Send them off to Philadelphia, New York, Connecticut and to Boston."[1]

Having had enough of the Acadians, British subjects who refused to sign the Oath of Allegiance, all was drawn to a dramatic halt on September 5, 1755, the very day when all Acadian men and boys over ten were ordered to show up at the church at Saint-Charles-des-Mines.

Madeleine had begged Michel to go into hiding so that they could carry through with their plan, but he refused, saying that it was a matter of principle, that family was the pillar of

[1] Landry, Peter. (2008). *History of Nova Scotia: Book 1, Part 6, Chapter 7: Acadia - The Deportation of the Acadians: The Deportation Orders* accessed on November 16, 2008 at http://www.blupete.com/Hist/NovaScotiaBk1/Part6/Ch07.htm

the community and that he needed to be there to support both his father and his brothers.

The women and daughters of the village knew nothing about this British plan, already in motion, so they continued to trust in good faith. Madeleine's heart was breaking because she knew what was to transpire.

Uncertain of the loyalty "of its Acadian subjects on the eve of an international war, Britain's colonial government in Nova Scotia ordered the deportation of the Acadians in 1755. In August, Colonel John Winslow and over 300 New England volunteers arrived at Grand-Pré to execute the government's orders. Winslow took command of the church at Saint-Charles-des-Mines, using the presbytery as his headquarters. After erecting a wooden palisade around his camp to 'prevent a surprise,' Winslow ordered all Acadian men and boys over the age of ten to attend a meeting at his camp at 3pm on September 5. Over four hundred showed up at the appointed hour to hear the king's wishes, only to be placed under arrest. The Deportation at Grand-Pré had officially begun." [2]

Needing an interpreter, John Winslow had summoned François Landry.

Gentlemen, I have received from his Excellency, Governor Lawrence, the King's instructions, which I have in my hands. By his orders you are called together to hear His Majesty's final resolution concerning the French inhabitants of this Province of Nova Scotia, who for more than a half century have had more indulgence granted them than any of his subjects in any part of his dominions. What use you have made of it, you yourselves best know.

The duty I am now upon, though necessary, is very disagreeable to my natural make and temper, as I know it must be grievous to you, who are of the same species.

---

[2] Northeast Archaeological Research. (2005). *Grand-Pré National Historic Site* accessed on November 16, 2008 at http://www.northeastarch.com/grand_pre.html

But it is not my business to dwell on the orders I have received, but to obey them and, therefore, without hesitation, I shall deliver to you His Majesty's instructions and commands, which are, that your lands and tenements and cattle and livestock of all kinds are forfeited to the crown, with all your effects, except money and household goods, and that you yourselves are to be removed from this Province.

The preemptory orders of His Majesty are, that all the French inhabitants of these Districts be removed, and through His Majesty's goodness, I am directed to allow you your money and as many of your household goods as you can take without overloading the vessels you go in. I shall do everything in my power that all these goods are secured to you and that you be not molested in carrying them away, and also that whole families shall go in the same vessel; so that this removal, which I am sensible must give you a great deal of trouble, may be made as easy as His Majesty's service will admit; and I hope that in whatever part of the world your lot may fall, you may be faithful subjects, and a peaceable and happy people.

I must also inform you, that it is His Majesty's pleasure that you remain in the security under inspection and direction of the troops that I have the honor to command.

John Winslow [3]

Landry was told that they would start the embarkation that day. It was Landry who was to read the orders that Winslow had written on that fateful day in the Saint-Charles-des-Mines church.

In retrospect, the men and boys were actually housed in the church for one month before the embarkation officially began. While it was indeed a blessing that the men and boys had been able to complete all that was required of them for the harvesting, it may well have been part of the overall plan. Had it been otherwise, the Acadian populace might have been able to deduce what was happening. Now they were being housed as political prisoners.

---

[3] *Winslow's Official Address to the imprisoned Acadians in the Grand Pré Church on September 5, 1755* accessed on November 26, 2011 at http://www.acadianmelancon.com/orders.html#announce

It was a month of excruciating uneasiness, especially for Madeleine, who was newly pregnant.

The promise made to the Acadians, that families were not to be divided during the process, was not kept. The motives of Charles Lawrence were not at all sympathetic to the plight of the Acadian people.

In a letter that was sent to Colonel Robert Monckton, he shared the following words ... "I would have you not wait for the wives and the children coming in but ship off the men without them." [4]

Over the course of several days, the women and children of the village continued to gather outside the church in a line that often went on for miles.

Unsure if their families were going to be kept intact, there was much lamentation and wailing.

---

[4] Griffiths, Naomi. *The Acadian Deportation: Causes and Development* Ph.D. thesis (p 176).

The last male to leave the church, Madeleine got her first glimpse of Michel in over a month. She could not believe how haggard and worn he looked; so much older than his actual years.

Madame Pêche quickly encouraged her to advance towards Michel, giving her a strange and secretive look. Needing no further bolstering, she ran to him, copious tears streaming down her face.

Amidst their misery and clasped hands, a young British soldier advanced towards them, placing his hand atop theirs in a genuine gesture of compassion and understanding. Looking quickly into his eyes, Madeleine realized how hard it must have been for him to have to follow such harsh orders.

Mere seconds later, Madeleine was overwhelmed by a sense of dizziness and nausea akin to déja-vu, fainting in a heap at the feet of the British soldier. Coming to, a few moments later, she found that she had been transported back to the Grand Pré of the twenty-first century, her time.

In actual fact, she quickly assessed it to be the very same day that her time travel experience first began.

Bereft at the loss of her love, and sobbing at the base of the statue of Evangeline, a young man in Acadian garb approached. Bending down, he was quick to offer her a handkerchief.

After having wiped her eyes, Madeleine discovered, to her complete astonishment, that the handkerchief presented to her, for her use, was the *same* one that she had lovingly weaved and embroidered for Michel.

Almost afraid to look up, she knew that she had no choice but to do so.

Their eyes met, hesitatingly at first.

Sharing a look of instant recognition, as well as momentary disbelief, tentative smiles quickly blossomed into wide grins as they fell into each other's arms, knowing that they had made it, knowing that their love was safe.

Chapter 1

Truly, I'm not sure what it was that propelled us forward in time. That very morning, Mother Pêche had *insisted* that I hide my back pack, complete with the copy of the Aramaic codex that Gabriel had so lovingly presented to me, along with the slim Latin volume, beneath my clothes.

She kept telling me that *the time had come* for Yeshua's book to be revealed. Perhaps, in truth, it was this relic of antiquity that had allowed for our return to the time from whence I'd come.

After taking a quick cursory look around the park, followed by a quick glance at her watch, Madeleine realized that they had about fifteen minutes before closure.

Back in the Acadie of 1755, she had done her best to prepare Michel for the twenty-first century, telling him as much as she could about the National Historic Site at Grand Pré, so that he wouldn't be completely overwhelmed upon their return.

She'd also shared with him the manner in which people lived in her time, including the various types of homes that existed, the modes of transportation utilized, and how they purchased both food and clothing items.

"Michel, the park is going to be closing in a few minutes, so we have to leave. We'll come back another time and stay as long as you'd like. The workers aren't going to suspect a thing; you have the most realistic look about you. Just keep holding my hand."

Now it was Michel's turn to try and get past the lump that had formed in his throat.

Mon dieu. I am really here. This is Grand Pré. I am really here in the twenty-first century with Madeleine.

While Michel was thrilled to be here with his wife, he missed his family in a deep and aching way, knowing that he would always wonder about what had happened to them.

Without a doubt, they were probably feeling the same about him.

Winslow had demanded that all the married and unmarried young men be separated, drawn up in columns.

Fathers had been separated from sons, brothers were separated from brothers. It was an absolutely horrific scene, soldiers advancing with bayonets in order to enforce the issued command. This was the scene that had greeted Madeleine that day.

In keeping with the tides of the Basin, the men were to be boarded on boats, traveling a distance of one and a half miles to the landing place on the Gaspereau, before finally being transported to the ships anchored there.

Many families had lined the road, watching the melancholy procession, falling on their knees to pray. Had Madeleine not chanced across Michel, thereby propelling him into the twenty-first century, what might have happened to him?

Had Michel's family been lucky enough to remain together?

Had they been torn asunder, never to find each other again?

Would they ever find answers to these questions?

Madeleine did her best to reassure Michel with a tender smile before pulling him along with her up the path.

After passing through the visitor's gates, they quickly made their way to her red four-door compact Honda Civic.

Madeleine pointed out which side of the car was his. Watching her open the car door, Michel attempted to do likewise, tugging on the chrome-colored handle. It wouldn't budge.

Walking around to his side of the car, she patiently showed him how to pull up on the handle and try to tug it towards him at the same time.

Making him try it several times, to be sure he could do it by himself, she waited for him to seat himself inside, before closing the door.

After relishing the comfort for a few moments, he turned to glance quizzically at Madeleine, as though to say, *What do I do now*.

"Michel, this is called a seat belt. It's made to stretch comfortably across the body, and buckles on the other side."

She put hers on and took it off; several times in fact, all the while explaining the process.

"It helps keep us safe while we're traveling anywhere by car."

Now it was Michel's turn to demonstrate that he knew what to do. He managed without a hitch.

Madeleine turned the key in the ignition. His eyes immediately met hers at the strange sound; she gave him a tired smile.

"Later, we'll worry about my teaching you how to drive. That's *really* going to be fun because this car is a standard. Right now, I just want to get home. If Mother Pêche was right, tomorrow will be my twenty-sixth birthday."

In the close to eight minutes that it took to drive from Grand Pré to her home in Gaspereau, Madeleine allowed Michel time to make peace with the dark thoughts that were residing within his soul. She knew that there'd be ample time to introduce him to her modern-day world.

Michel, frightened out of his wits, gripped both sides of his seat with whitened knuckles, hanging on as if his very life depended on it. In reality, it did. Closing his eyes to combat the dizziness he was experiencing, he prayed as he never had before.

Chapter 2

The next morning, Madeleine awoke, completely refreshed after her deep sleep. Finding herself in her own comfortable bed was a most reassuring feeling. To confirm that she wasn't dreaming, she pinched the skin of her arm. *Oh, that hurts.* Almost immediately, she let go.

She lay quietly, so as not to disturb Michel, remembering that this was her twenty-sixth birthday. In her estimation, having her beloved Michel here to celebrate with her on this special day, and in her own time, was the most precious gift to be had.

Her fingers quickly found the simple wedding band on her left hand. How was she going to explain this to her mother?

Oh, my goodness. Mother told me that she would be here around mid-afternoon to help me celebrate my birthday.

That's when Madeleine leaped out of bed, running to the bathroom.

Knowing that her day was about to begin at a frantic pace, she quickly stepped into the shower, so glad to be able to lather the Paula's Choice All-Over Hair and Body Shampoo just the way that she liked, courtesy of her shower puff.

During her stay in Acadie, she had come to miss this particular luxury.

Wrapping her hair in a turban and her body in a thick towel, she emerged from the bath to find Michel stirring. He was being inundated with so many things at once, that she was beginning to wonder whether he'd be able to accept all the changes facing him.

Let's just get through this day, she thought to herself before quickly donning a pair of jeans and a tee-shirt. She gave a deep sigh of satisfaction.

Clothing comfort had been a long time coming.

The sound of the blow dryer made Michel bolt upright in the bed, resulting in a painful smack to his forehead, courtesy of the sharply-slanted ceiling. He fell back onto his pillow, groaning.

This is going to be a long day, a day that is going to feel like forever were his first coherent thoughts as he ran his finger gently over the lump already forming above his brow. He sighed.

Slowly, Michel crawled off the bed and stood in one spot on the floor until the dizziness passed and the horrible pain in his head receded to a dull drumbeat. It was only upon entering the bathroom that he was able to track the source of the most infuriating noise.

"Good morning, Michel. Did you sleep well?"

Michel gawked at his wife in her hip-hugging jeans and form-fitting tee-shirt.

Is this how people dress in this new world he asked himself, while nodding his head to answer his wife's question.

If it was hard enough looking at his wife dressed like this, how was he ever going to get by without staring outright, at everyone he would come to meet?

Noticing his wide-eyed stare, Madeleine could do nothing but giggle. Mere moments later, they were both engulfed in stomach-holding laughter.

Yes, this was going to take much acclimatizing. Madeleine was unsure how he would react when interesting hair styles, hair colors, body piercings and tattoos got added to the mix.

She began to introduce Michel to the modern convenience of a shower and a toilet. Suffice it to say that he was completely mesmerized.

"I cannot believe that there are so many major differences between my time and yours," he said.

Showing him how to use the toilet was the first step. Next came the flushing. How was it that a simple flick of the wrist could make everything disappear?

He kept turning the water faucets on and off, as Madeleine showed him. Afterwards, she encouraged him to step into the bathtub and showed him how to operate the shower.

This resulted in a rather large bellow from Michel, followed by a giggle from Madeleine, before he was able to relax enough to enjoy his first modern-day shower.

Michel now knew how to open a car door, fasten a seat belt, flush a toilet and take a shower. *Four down, a million more to go*, thought Madeleine, smiling inwardly.

Rather than have him shop with her, wearing his Acadian attire, she would simply make note of his measurements after breakfast, before rushing off, alone, to Mark's Work Warehouse.

Eager to get back into her own kitchen, Madeleine made Bob's Red Mill Organic Scottish Oatmeal for breakfast. After their trek back through time, they needed something warm and nourishing.

She showed him where the milk and filtered water were kept.

"Why do you keep your food in such a big box?" he asked his wife.

"To keep them cool and fresh," she replied.

"How can this box do that?"

Not prepared for a long explanation of electricity and the cooling and freezing qualities of the refrigerator, Madeleine said, "I'll explain later," encouraging Michel to enjoy his hot oatmeal. Not long thereafter, she was heading for the door with his measurements in one hand and her car keys in the other.

She turned back long enough to turn on the television, showing Michel how to operate the remote. While she was not an avid TV fan, this was surely the device to keep him entertained until her return. Seldom did she thank her lucky stars for cable, but this was one such time.

"I'll be back as soon as I've bought the clothes that you need," she said. "We'll get there, one step at a time."

After giving him a quick kiss on the forehead, the very spot that had suffered harsh contact with the slanted ceiling, and directing him to the fruit basket filled with bananas, apples and pears, she was gone.

She could see that, being too distracted by the magic of the TV, he hadn't been paying attention to her anyway. She smiled as she headed to the car.

The trip to Mark's took much longer than expected, but Madeleine was quite satisfied with what she had been able to purchase for Michel – several pairs of jeans, two acid wash and one black (for a dressier look), a leather belt for durability, boxer shorts, tee-shirts, several dress shirts and a black leather tie (to complete the more formal look with the jeans), as well as a pair of Nike running shoes. Two pairs of leather loafers, one pair black and the other tan, were added to the pile, simply because she couldn't make up her mind about the color.

No one she knew had chanced across her as she completed finding and paying for men's clothing items, so she was able to leave the store as soon as she'd finished.

How would she be able to explain the wedding band on her left hand to friends, colleagues and acquaintances, when she was yet to come up with a suitable story for her mother?

One thing she knew, for sure, she was beat and the day had barely started.

After leaving the store, she decided to get a few groceries as well. Thank goodness a friend had filled her freezer with a large supply of venison last winter.

She could now concentrate on purchasing fresh vegetables, fruit and homemade bread. After adding a few more items to her cart, chocolate being one, she paid the bill and headed for home.

She smiled to herself as she sped out of the parking lot. Since her marriage to Michel, albeit on this very day in 1755, Madeleine felt that any house, in which she and her husband were living, was going to feel like home.

She was more than ready to begin their life together. She was *not*, however, ready to deal with the sight that greeted her upon her return.

Chapter 3

Merde was the first word that came to mind when she saw her mother's vehicle parked in the yard. For the very first time, Madeleine was now wishing that she hadn't given her mother a key to the house.

Sitting for a few moments in the parked Civic, she did her best to try and collect her thoughts.

Knowing that Kathleen Sinclair, known as Kate to her dearest and closest friends, was one for taking charge of any given situation, Madeleine knew that there was no coming up with a plan at this point.

Feeling as though she had just tumbled down the rabbit hole, she commanded herself to remain calm.

"It's okay, Madeleine. You're going to be fine. Just take several deep breaths. In, out. That's it. In, out."

Taking the key out of the ignition, she grabbed the bags and headed up the walkway, key in hand.

Before she could insert the key into the lock, her mother opened the door. She greeted Madeleine with a strange look on her face.

Oh, dear, here it comes. I'm in for it now.

Here she was, today at twenty-six, feeling like that gawky, sixteen-year-old again, with her first boyfriend.

"Maddie, dearest, it seems yesterday's sojourn at Grand Pré was a resounding success, with a new husband in tow. Your Michel has been quite the entertaining host in your absence."

Madeleine felt the uncertainty building with each word that continued to issue forth from her mother's lips.

"Hi, Mom, would you be kind enough to put these groceries away for me, please, while I see to Michel?"

She placed the bags of food on the kitchen table and leaning close to her mother, whispered, "We'll talk later, okay?"

“Not a problem, dear. You go see to Michel so we can all sit down, in a few moments, with a fresh cup of coffee as we discuss the situation.”

Madeleine practically raced to the bedroom with the bags from Mark’s.

No doubt about it, lounging on the bed in her fuschia robe, with his dark hair and swarthy dark looks, he did cut quite the dashing sight.

“Madeleine, I thought I was shocked when I found myself here in the twenty-first century, but your mother, when she arrived ...”

“Say no more, Michel. I know exactly what you’re trying to tell me. She can be rather overbearing at times, with her take-charge attitude, but she really is the kindest Mom anyone could ever want, and I love her dearly.”

She grinned mischievously.

"However, I must say that you make a very delightful picture in my robe. Come over here and take a look for yourself."

Standing beside the full-length mirror, she guided him to stand directly in front of it.

He nodded, "Yes, I see what you mean, Madeleine. It makes me wonder what Maman would say if she could see me dressed like this?"

Turning from side to side, as if admiring himself from every angle, he continued. "I must admit, this is a most fetching color, is it not?"

Madeleine burst into giggles. "Come on, let's get you fitted with some real clothes. I'm sure that you'll find them very comfortable."

The boxer shorts were a breeze. Michel even commented on how acceptable they felt. Next, Madeleine handed him a white tee-shirt and pair of acid-wash jeans, demonstrating how the zipper worked.

"Make sure you tuck in your tee-shirt before you zip up your jeans."

Michel left the bathroom to look at himself in the mirror, taking stock of every individual piece, as he put it on.

He wasn't too sure about the zipper, but after a couple of tries, and a few swear words, he managed. The jeans fit him very well.

Having never shopped for a male before, Madeleine was duly impressed with her shopping efforts. *This will be a first of many*, *I'm sure*, were her thoughts as she added the leather belt, the final finishing touch, before redirecting him toward the mirror.

Dark indigo-blue eyes, framing the darkest, longest, curliest eyelashes that Madeleine had ever seen on a male, stared back at her.

Madeleine appreciated how the white tee-shirt enhanced his sun-kissed skin, further accentuated his white teeth, and framed the muscular arms. Not being a narcissistic man, Michel just stared at his reflection in complete silence.

He was astounded at how much clothing could change the look of a person. While there was nothing about them that *looked* out of place, he still *felt* so out of place. Confusion filled his eyes.

His hand reached out to grasp Madeleine's. She drew him into her warm, comforting embrace, holding him tightly until the tension began to leave his eyes and his body relaxed.

"As awkward as I feel at this very moment *chérie*, I know we are going to be fine. Come."

He held out his hand to her.

"I am sure your mother is waiting for an explanation from us. We must not keep her waiting any longer."

Chapter 4

Michel emerged from the bedroom with more confidence than Madeleine herself was feeling. She could feel her heart begin to race from the anxiety that was building. Giving her fingers a gentle squeeze, Michel smiled reassuringly as they walked into the kitchen.

Just look at him. He's so calm. Why doesn't he feel the anxiety that I'm feeling, she wondered. *I feel like giving him a good poke.*

As they neared the kitchen, a look of firm resolve spread over her face, replacing the uncertainty; they were, after all, in this together.

Kate had put the groceries away and was just finishing the last of the breakfast dishes. The smell of freshly-brewed coffee filled the air, something else that Madeleine had clearly missed.

Placing some decadent-smelling chocolate chip cookies on a plate, Kate directed everyone to the kitchen table before advancing towards the coffee maker.

"Sit down, Mom," Madeleine said. "I'll get the coffee."

She waved her mother to a chair. Kate gratefully sat down. Placing the carafe on the trivet in the middle of the table, she brought over the sugar dish, the fresh milk (in the carton) and several teaspoons, before sitting beside Michel.

"Thanks for the birthday cookies, Mom. You don't know how much I've missed them. I really need my chocolate fix today."

Pouring coffee into three mugs, she placed all of them in the center of the table.

"Help yourselves to the milk and sugar."

A funny look came over Michel's face when he picked up the milk and proceeded to pour some into his coffee.

"How does the milk manage to stay so cool and fresh in this little box?"

Kate gave Madeleine a look that clearly, and loudly, spoke volumes; something was definitely wrong with Michel.

Madeleine ignored the look on her mother's face and smiled at Michel.

"That's another of those things I'll have to explain at a later time, Michel. Let's just enjoy these cookies and our coffee for now."

Michel nodded slowly, not understanding the delay, but willing to shut down his curiosity for the moment.

Kate continued to wait patiently, while Madeleine spent a few moments sipping her coffee and collecting her thoughts.

Finally she sighed, glancing at her mother before beginning.

"There's no easy way to say what I have to say, except to just come out and say it. Yes, Michel and I are husband and wife. We were married on my twenty-sixth birthday in 1755."

There. It was out, finally.

"Maddie, come now. What kind of a tale are you spinning me? You know it was just yesterday that you were part of the Acadian festivities at Grand Pré."

Kate sighed deeply. "Not only that, but you hadn't even been dating anyone, unless you were doing so in secret and had not yet had a chance to tell me."

Kate's eyes widened, as an immediate thought came to mind. "Were you forced into it? Oh, my God, you're not pregnant, are you?"

It was now Michel's turn to sigh.

"Kate, if I may speak freely. Madeleine is telling you the complete truth. She traveled from 2005, her time, to mine, arriving on August 16, 1754. It was one year to the day later that we were married. This must seem strange to anyone from this time, knowing that Madeleine is just twenty-six today. It seems that a whole year in my time was not even one full day in yours."

Michel continued, nodding to Madeleine and her mother.

"Three days after we were married, the British came to Grand Pré. Marching into the center of town, Lieutenant Colonel John Winslow quickly took possession of our parish church, Saint-Charles-des-Mines, using it as his base camp. He ordered his men to build a palisade [5] for their defense, a plan that had been well thought out, given the earlier battle at Grand Pré, between the British and the French, in 1747.

"All of the men and boys over the age of ten, were ordered to report to the church on September 5 at 3:00 in the afternoon. After the royal proclamation was read, we were confined to the church. Madeleine tells me that we became political prisoners."

Michel paused, taking a few breaths before continuing.

"In total, there were four hundred eighteen unsuspecting souls. Madeleine wanted me to go into hiding, but I refused. That would have been most cowardly of me. We were

---

[5] Société Promotion Grand-Pré. *Archaeology: Site Report* accessed on December 24, 2008 at http://www.grand-pre.com/GrandPreSiteDevelopment/en/SiteReport.html

detained inside the church for an entire month before they began the embarkation, one group at a time.

“If you believe Madeleine to have lost her mind, and to be insane, than I sit here before you, ready to be condemned, thusly, as well.”

It never ceased to amaze Madeleine that Michel was able to converse in both languages with equal fluency. She simply had to ask. “How did you learn to speak English so well?”

Michel shifted his attention to his wife.

“Mother Pêche was teaching me, preparing me for a time when she said that I would need to know the language. When we first began our lessons, I thought this role might, have been connected with the coming of the British, and, as it appears, I was right, but I never questioned her motives.

“She also took the time to teach me how to read and write English as well, stressing their importance in the future. Not for one moment did I think that she meant this time in your world. I am truly so grateful to her for having done so.”

At this point, Kate spoke up.

"Now I am even more confused; just who is this Mother Pêche?"

Madeleine was quick to provide the answer.

"Mother Pêche, a time-traveler like me, like us," she nodded to her husband, "was our saving grace. Knowing what happened to Michel and me, I am now of the impression that parallel universes exist, universes in which one can travel backward, as well as forward, on a time continuum. Just because we can't see it, just because we haven't experienced it, doesn't mean that it doesn't exist.

"It could be said that we are all time-travelers. For example, as you sit at your desk doing nothing more than clicking the mouse, 'time is traveling around you. The future is constantly being transformed into the past, with the present only lasting for a fleeting moment. Everything that you are doing right now is quickly moving into the past, which means we continue to move through time.' [6] This is something that I have never given any credence to, until now. While I can't tell you how it happened, I can only tell you that it did."

Madeleine sighed tiredly, relieved to have her story begun. Michel gave his wife a reassuring hug.

Madeleine stood up, mug in one hand and the plate of cookies in the other, while saying, "Let's take our coffee into the living-room, shall we?"

She started for the hallway, without even so much as a backwards glance to see if they were following her; she'd just assumed they would.

---

[6] Bonsor, Kevin. (1998). HowStuffWorks, Inc. (1998). *How Time Travel Works* accessed on December 25, 2008 at http://science.howstuffworks.com/time-travel.htm

Chapter 5

Michel quickly joined Madeleine in the love seat. She gave him a quick smile, waiting until her mother was seated comfortably on the adjacent sofa, before taking a deep breath.

"You remember, Mom, how hard I'd been working, doing my best to create an authentic Acadian costume that I could wear to the Acadian Day celebrations at Grand Pré. What a wonderful day it was. They taught us the words to several Acadian songs, and we danced until we nearly wore out our shoes, or so it felt. There were showings of arts and crafts from local entrepreneurs as well as workshops that featured the making of crafts, painting and even the building of dykes. Finally, there was a challenging treasure hunt, made all the more difficult because we weren't permitted to use any kind of a GPS device.

"To tempt the taste buds, there were traditional Acadian dishes and other culinary treats. I loved the corn soup, all the while thinking how easy it would be to make for myself;

of course, the Clam Fricot was another popular choice. Eating the meat pie made me think about those delicious venison pies of Granny's that we loved to eat throughout the winter. Everything was wonderful, except for the small sampling of Dandelion wine, offered only, of course, to those of legal drinking age. I was completely unable to stomach the taste.

"Acadians, and Acadians at heart, had eagerly gathered to have fun and celebrate together. It was towards the end of the day, as festivities had drawn to a close, and almost everyone had left the park grounds, that I made one more visit to see Evangeline. After a day of wonderment and enjoyment, it seemed that she and I had made a deeper connection.

"Without knowing the why of it all, I began to cry. In an attempt to convey my emotional thoughts to her, I reached up to stroke the folds of her dress. It was at that moment that I was overcome with a foreboding sense of dizziness and nausea, fainting at the base of the statue, and waking up in, what seemed to be, the space of a few minutes."

Madeleine paused, taking a sip of her still-hot coffee and then nibbling on a cookie, as if for added sustenance.

"I woke up to complete darkness and found that I was quite disoriented, unable to stand at my first attempt. My head felt very heavy and woozy. After several moments of slow, deep and focused breathing, I was able to sit up without that heavy fogginess in my brain.

"I wondered why nobody at the park noticed me. As soon as that thought came to me, that's when I *knew* that something didn't feel right, that the air felt different, that the air smelled different. I stood up in an effort to get my bearings in the dark."

She glanced at her mother.

"I kept thinking about how you would always tell me that I was like a cat on the prowl after dark because nothing seemed to inhibit my superior night vision. The hair on my arms immediately stood up on end and I experienced a deep, deep chill to the bone. I just knew that there was no way that I could still be at the park.

"Everything had disappeared from view, except for one building that was close by; it seemed so surreal, like a strange dream.

"Walking across the ground, quickly covering the short distance to the building, I entered to discover what looked like a church, but one that didn't even come close to resembling the church on the park grounds at Grand Pré. There was nothing smooth to the touch about the wood. The metal handle on the door reminded me of the same type that was on the outhouse door at Granny's; that's why I had no difficulty entering.

"There were no pictures on the walls, no adornments of any kind. I found myself walking gingerly toward what seemed to resemble pews. Overcome with exhaustion, made even more intense by not knowing where it was that I had found myself, I sat down.

"Reaching into my trusty back pack, I found the survival packet containing the blanket that always reminds me of a gigantic piece of aluminum foil; the one you are always reminding me to take on my spontaneous hikes. Well, after positioning the back pack as a pillow and tucking the blanket around and under my body, I fell into a deep sleep.

"Unbeknownst to me, Madame Péche had been following me. She, too, had quietly entered the building. I have no idea how long I actually slept, just that when I dug my watch out of my back pack to see the time, it was 3:33 AM."

Madeleine paused, taking another few sips of coffee. At that specific mention of time, Kate smiled. Madeleine had been privy to these types of numeral combinations, with favorable results, all her life.

"You know me, Mom, wide awake and ready to explore my environment, I folded the aluminum-foil blanket, stowed it in my back pack before turning to leave the church. That's when I came to realize that I was not alone. I gave a scream and fell back down, giving myself a rather good smack on the back of my head. This woman came over to me and started talking in French. I did my best to let her know that I wasn't French, that I couldn't speak French. That was when she started speaking to me in English, telling me her name was Madame Péche.

"When she told me that she had been *expecting* me, well, I began thinking that maybe she was suffering from Alzheimer's or some other type of mental illness. There was simply no way that she could've been expecting me. While she had introduced herself as Madame Péche, she also told me that this wasn't her real name.

"All of a sudden, I felt like someone living in the twilight zone. For the first time I began to feel afraid; I didn't know where I was and yet I was housed in this building with a woman who might be completely insane.

"I asked her to tell me what year it was. No one could have been more stupified at her response, than me, when she told me that it was August 16, 1754. That's when she welcomed me to Grand Pré, calling me by name. I started to shake and couldn't stop; even my teeth began to chatter.

"In all honesty, I paid not one iota of attention to anything else as I followed her, which wasn't normal for me.

"Dad had always stressed the importance of taking note of my surroundings, which is such an important aspect of survivalist training, as you well know, Mom.

"I can't tell you how far we walked or how long it took. I can't even tell you the direction that we traveled. I just felt such a rush of adrenaline that everything else faded into the background amidst my throbbing temples.

"When we entered her small home, I took notice of the crude and sparse furnishings. Madame prepared a small fire in the hearth. It seems that I couldn't stop shaking. As soon as she informed me that I had, indeed, spent the night inside the original parish church of Saint-Charles-des-Mines, I realized that I'd traveled back in time, some 250 years, going from August 15, 2005 to August 16, 1754."

Madeleine was starting to feel chilled, so Michel went off in search of something warm, returning a few moments later with some woolen socks, a sweater and a blanket.

"Mom, this Madame Péche knew *everything* there was to know about me.

"She knew my birthday, she knew my name, she even knew the year I was born. However, what upset me the most was the fact that she knew about my birthmark."

At these words, Kate, herself, shuddered.

"But how is that even possible, Maddie? It just makes no sense."

"Sense or not, I can't explain it except to say that she was an incredibly gifted and highly intuitive woman. That was when she proceeded to tell me a story about the Sinclairs. Let's just say that my having read The Da Vinci Code, and other related titles, was my way of synthesizing all of the information that she shared. Even Michel, in the very beginning, was not privy to what she disclosed to me."

Michel gave her a comforting hug.

Knowing that they were going to be here chatting, probably long into the evening, it was Kate who suggested that they place an order at Pizza Delight instead of going out.

Madeleine readily agreed, knowing that Michel was going to be bombarded with a mélange of tastes and food textures.

Between garlic fingers, Greek style pizza with extra feta cheese as well as white sauce, caesar salad with real bacon pieces and crunchy croutons, it was going to be a veritable feast.

Kate left to pick it up, giving Madeleine and Michel some much needed time alone.

Chapter 6

Kate returned about forty minutes later. Neither Madeleine nor Michel realized just how hungry they were until she'd returned, ringing the doorbell, with food in hand.

Mouth-watering odors emanated from the packages she carried. Michel quickly relieved his mother-in-law of the boxes and bags in her hands. Kate sighed in relief.

"They seem to be getting heavier than I remembered," she said to her daughter.

Maddie laughed. "That's because we usually have everything delivered, Mom."

Kate rolled her eyes. "Before we delve any further into this remarkable story," she said, "let's eat. I need significant nourishment, something better and more filling than coffee and cookies."

"I agree," replied Michel, and, as if on cue, his stomach made a loud rumbling noise.

Everyone laughed as they hurried towards the kitchen where Michel deposited the pizza boxes and the salad containers on the counter top.

Holding her arms out to her daughter, and wishing her a Happy Birthday, she encouraged Michel to join them for a group hug, after which Kate directed Madeleine and Michel to the table and quickly served the salad.

Madeleine liked to think of herself as a caesar salad connoisseur of sorts. With a tendency to order this salad everywhere she went, no one came close to making it the way she liked it, à la Pizza Delight.

While Michel was familiar with romaine lettuce and bacon, the croutons and parmesan cheese were a totally foreign taste to him. Likewise for the roasted garlic in olive oil and salty anchovy taste. The dressing was smooth and creamy. Madeleine showed him that he could squeeze the lemon wedge over the salad, if he wished.

Letting the flavors meld in his mouth, Michel sighed with outright pleasure.

Madeleine watched him eat every speck on his plate. *He's taking to these new foods like a duck takes to water*, she thought.

"This is absolutely heavenly, if indeed that is a word that can be associated with food. What do you call this?"

"This, my dearest, is caesar salad. You are quite right, you know; heavenly is the very word that I've often used to describe the taste. However, just wait until you've tried the garlic fingers and the Greek style pizza before you tell us which one is your favorite."

Michel deemed the garlic fingers to be passable in taste, but it was the Greek style pizza with the tangy feta cheese, along with the caesar salad, that won the day.

"Now *that* is a taste to live for, is it not? What do you think, Kate?"

"I have to agree with you, Michel. You've hit on two of our favorite foods."

Munching their fill until they were sated, Kate was the first to arise from the table to rinse the dishes before putting on a fresh pot of coffee.

"You, two, go relax. I'll take care of the dishes and bring the coffee in when it's ready."

"Thanks, Mom. I really appreciate it." Madeleine gave her a quick hug before leading the way to the living room.

"Yes, thank you, Kate. Everything was delicious." Michel was quick to follow his wife.

Kate smiled at her retreating son-in-law, still mesmerized by the fact that their marriage was a reality. Clearly this was one of the most fascinating tales to which she'd ever been privy.

It wasn't that she didn't, or couldn't, believe, for there had been countless synchronicities of a mystic nature in her own life. It was simply a matter of never having before been presented with surrealism of such an intense, and powerful, quality, making it feel as if one's last hold on sanity was being blown out of the water.

She was at a complete loss for words, coupled with the fact that her daughter was the most honest person she knew. There was no way that Maddie could have made up such a story, no matter how remarkable.

If I am feeling this way, so completely overwhelmed, I can only begin to imagine how Madeleine and Michel must be feeling.

Arranging everything on a carrying tray, Kate entered the living room.

"Okay, my one and only daughter, let's drink our coffee and continue, shall we? As hard as it for me to get a solid grasp on all that you're sharing here, I *know* that you are the most honest, most courteous, most considerate person, that I've ever had the pleasure of knowing, so let's just continue to take this tale one step at a time."

"Thank you for validating our experiences, Kate. That means so much to Madeleine and me."

Taking a small sip of coffee, Madeleine was quick to return to her story.

"It was clear that Madame Pêche was able to converse with the best when it came to the spoken word. This very worldly, highly intelligent, woman told me such an incredible story about my Sinclair line, that it was almost too much for me to fathom.

"She told me that I had been propelled backwards in time because it was my destiny to be there, to become apprenticed, if you will, under her care.

"Sinclair, she told me, is a form of St. Clair, a name that means *Shining Light*. Having delved into father's genealogy, I knew that the first St. Clair was Rollo the Viking, father of William Longsword. I also knew about William de St. Clair, the one we call the Conqueror. It was this illegitimate son of Robert II de St. Clair, Duke of Normandy, who fought at Hastings in 1066, emerging victorious to become King William I of England.

"Madame Péche spoke to me about Henry Sinclair, 1st Earl of Orkney, Baron of Roslin and Lord of Shetland, traveling to the New World in 1398. She also told me about William Sinclair, 1st Earl of Caithness, the grandson, who commissioned the building of Rosslyn Chapel in Scotland in 1446."

Kate acknowledged the connection with a shiver.

"I remember that you just had to see Rosslyn Chapel for yourself after having read The Da Vinci Code, although you didn't know why. Even though your father was sick at the time, he gave you his blessing to go to Scotland. I think he regretted not having shared the family history with you. Indeed, I believe you went there for both of you."

Madeleine, in complete agreement with her mother's viewpoint, nodded. "Knowing that I'd been there seemed to make his passing so much more peaceful," she said.

"He was delighted with the pictures that I brought back for him to hold. It was through his estate that I bought this house and property, for which I will always be thankful. You know me, Mom. I've always been one to need my own space."

Both mother and daughter took a few moments to reminisce.

"I hadn't known that Henry was a patron of refugee Templars, a group that had been created by the kings of Jerusalem. What I did know, however, was that these Templar Knights were reputed to have been the guardians of the Holy Grail.

"Madame then shared a fact of considerable importance. She told me that a great many researchers and scholars, then as well as now, believe the Holy Grail to have been "a code phrase describing the descendants of Jesus, the Holy Bloodline, that was a living vessel in which the Holy Blood was held, preserved, and perpetuated." [7]

Madeleine paused, taking another sip of deliciously hot coffee before continuing.

"She also disclosed that it may have been the Holy Grail that was evacuated from the last Cathar stronghold in 1244,

---

[7] Mann, William F. (2004). *The Knights Templar in the New World: How Henry Sinclair Brought the Grail to Acadia* (p. xi). Rochester, VT: Destiny Books.

spirited away from the doomed Montségur by three knights just a few days before the citadel surrendered." [8]

Kate took in a surprised breath.

"I know, Mom. This totally captivated me, too, knowing how much I resonate with Montségur and the Cathars. She went on to state that if, as Cathar tradition suggests, the Holy Grail was actually "a lineage of people descended from Jesus and Mary Magdalene, and if the scions of this Holy Bloodline were actually saved from Montségur, then these Holy Blood descendants, along with a fair number of Templar protectors, may well have ended up in Scotland with Henry Sinclair." [9] I was totally unprepared for this revelation.

"For some reason, I just couldn't stop shivering when she talked about Montségur; this will be the very next place that

---

[8] Mann, William F. (2004). *The Knights Templar in the New World: How Henry Sinclair Brought the Grail to Acadia* (p. xi). Rochester, VT: Destiny Books.
[9] Ibid, p. xiii.

I visit. She told me that ours was a clan whose motto was *Commit thy work to God*, which was why I was there.

“I can remember looking at her, most strangely, when she said that. However, it wasn’t until she told me that I was the *first female*, born of a long and uninterrupted line of St. Clair males, from 911 AD to 1979, to bear a very special birthmark, above my left breast, the one that looks like a Templar cross … that I knew she was reaching the crux of her message. She kept insisting, over and over again, that I was ‘the one’. When I asked her about it, all she would say was that I was there to reclaim that which had been lost for many years, sharing such with the world.”

“I am surmising that you now know what that might be,” Kate interjected.

“I know, yes, but Michel does not, and we shall get to that later. Madame told me the Cathari treasure that was secreted away, down the mountain and across the French crusade lines, while most valuable then, is *still* of significant eminence today.

"You see, the treasure was actually tri-fold. Yeshua had two wives, a most acceptable position for a Jewish Rabbi of his day. He was first married to Miriam (of Bethany of the House of Saul) [10] as has clearly been alluded to in the Bible. While things have a tendency to get a tad murky, once Mirium (of the House of Æthiopia) known as Magdalene [11] is added to the equation, it really need not, for, you see, she was his second wife.

"The Cathari treasure that was secreted down the mountain of Montségur was [1] a direct female descendant of the Elchasai line, courtesy of Miriam of Bethany, [2] a direct female descendant connected with the Æthiopian connection, courtesy of Mirium Magdalene, and [3] a copy of a book as written by Yeshua himself.

---

[10] Montgomery, Hugh. (2006). *The God-Kings of Europe: The Descendants of Jesus Traced Through the Odonic and Davidic Dynasties* (p. 32). San Diego, CA: The Book Tree.
[11] Ibid.

"All were transported, safely and discreetly, to the isle of Scotland, leaving La Rochelle, France, in the wee hours of Friday, October 13, 1307.

"One of the knights, entrusted with the safe-keeping of the treasure, was a direct descendant of Bertrand de Blanchefort, the sixth Grand Master of the Knights Templar. He was a direct male descendant, meaning from father to son to son to son, from the Merovingian lineage. Most importantly, he was the ancestor of Michel. Another important fact is that Michel bears the same birthmark as me, but upon his right breast."

It was at this disclosure that Kate spilled her coffee.

"I think I can figure out where this is going, even with the little bit of knowledge that I'd been able to glean from you about The Da Vinci Code and its connection with your trip to Rosslyn. Give me a few moments to wipe up this spilled coffee."

With that, she practically ran to the kitchen for a cloth.

Kate's heart was racing. She knew that it was her turn to practice focused breathing for a few moments before returning to the living room. With a concerned look on his face, Michel was quick to join her a few moments later.

"It is a lot to take in, I know. I can remember how I felt at first. While I cannot be sure how much Madame actually intended to share, there came a time when she knew she had no choice but to tell me everything. By that time, we had known each other for nine years, and I had taken to calling her Mother Péche, like an adopted son, you could say. It took some time for me be able to digest the information."

"You can say that again."

Michel stood there with a confused look on his face.

"Yes, I suppose that I could, if you were to insist, but that would be a tad silly, would it not?"

Kate burst into peals of laughter.

Quickly she explained what the expression meant, pleased when she saw that the confusion in Michel's eyes soon changed to understanding.

"Thank you, Michel. While you wouldn't have known, this was exactly what I needed. Let's get back to Maddie."

With the spill already taken care of, Madeleine waited until everyone was seated. Looking first at Michel, and then at Kate, she continued.

"Remembering the knights who traveled with their treasure to Scotland, it was there that they found refuge with the Sinclair family. The de Blanchefort knight married the direct female descendant connected with the Æthiopian line. It is their very blood that courses through Michel.

"Long has the Sinclair family been noted as being the protectors of the Holy Grail. It was into this very family that the direct female descendant, connected with the Elchasai line, married. It is thought that Elchasai was a title, perhaps meaning *Higher Power*. It is her blood that courses through my veins.

"So, you see, Mom, both Michel and I are direct descendants of Yeshua."

Madeleine paused to gather her thoughts, before continuing.

"It was then that Madame presented the new metaphysical equation, and one of sublime simplicity at that, for her words were: '*your Sinclair line, meaning 'Shining Light' added to Michel's LeBlanc (de Blanchefort) line, meaning 'House of Light' or 'Fortress of Light' is the much needed merger to bring back that which was once lost to the world. In order to complete this mission, you must both return to your time in the twenty-first century world.*' Suffice it to say that I was absolutely mesmerized. Here was this elderly woman, of miraculous ability, telling me that Michel and I were going to be the ones to perpetuate the lineage, and I'd only just arrived on the scene."

Kate chose her words with great care.

"If the two of you are direct descendants, what is it that you have reclaimed to share with the world?"

All of a sudden, Michel knew *exactly* what it was.

"It is the third part of the treasure. It has something to do with the book that Yeshua himself wrote, the one that was secreted down the mountain of Montségur, yes?"

Madeleine turned toward Michel with an expansive smile.

"You are so very right, Michel. In fact, I think it may well be this treasure, this relic of antiquity if you will, that enabled us to return to my time."

Madeleine's eyes quickly filled with tears, her smile quickly replaced with a most tumultuous look.

"That very morning that I went to see you at the church, among the men and boys who were being separated, there was so much anguish, so much desolation.

"While we had attempted, for several days, to get a chance to see you, it was Mother Pêche who *insisted* that I hide my back pack, complete with the copy of the Aramaic codex, along with the slim Latin volume, beneath my clothes that very morning.

"I can still hear Gabriel telling me that the time had come for Yeshua's book to be revealed. Since having undressed last night before falling into bed, I've not had time to delve into my back pack. Why don't you get it for me while I find the latex gloves."

Chapter 7

While Madeleine placed a cotton blanket across the dining room table, Michel brought out the back pack that certainly looked no worse for wear, in spite of having spent a year in Madame's home.

After unzipping the bag, she peered inside. Expecting two packages, she was surprised to discover several others. What could they possibly be?

Starting with the biggest package, she untied the cord. After unwrapping soft deer hide, no doubt a gift from Gabriel, she discovered a hand-woven linen veil, embroidered with delicate pink and red roses.

Immediately overcome with emotion, Madeleine needed some time to compose herself before advancing to the next package.

Kate patted her daughter's hand. "This is absolutely beautiful, Maddie. I can understand why you're so emotional about it."

After wiping away a few tears, Madeleine responded.

"No, Mom, it's actually more than that. It was Madame herself that taught me how to weave this linen veil. I made, and embroidered, this piece, wearing it on the day that Michel and I were married."

Woven from flax, the strongest of vegetable fibers, Madeleine knew that this piece would be one to retain its strength and durability for many years to come. She held it lovingly to her breast.

"You looked so elegant that day; none could rival your beauty." Michel drew his wife into his arms, kissing the top of her head. He gestured to her wedding veil. "You were clearly not expecting to see this ever again. Let us see what else Mother Pêche took the care to pack for us."

Upon lifting the veil carefully from the package, Madeleine was pleasantly surprised to find their marriage document, complete with signatures. She handled it gently, knowing that it would need to be preserved for posterity.

“Now that, dearest Maddie, is a treasure beyond value, one that you won’t be able to share with too many people, I suspect.”

“I agree, Mom. It’s enough that we, three, have seen it.”

Eager to inspect the contents of the remaining packages, the very next one turned out to be the Aramaic codex written by Yeshua. Madeleine quickly suggested they all put on the latex gloves.

“I’m still finding it hard to believe that cousin Gabriel so easily entrusted this to me, saying that he’d always known a time would come, in his future, when he would be passing it on to another of the Sinclair line.

“Mom, this is the very book, written by Yeshua in Aramaic, the one that Gabriel stated was to be shared with the citizens of the world, the world of our time. He also instructed me to have its authenticity validated and verified.

“There is a smaller volume, in another package, that contains the Latin translation of this Aramaic text.

"It was from this particular translation that Madame was able to provide a third volume, translated directly from Latin into French. She knew how easy it would be to translate the work, from French, into many other languages, so that the message of Yeshua could easily reach one and all.

"Gabriel also told me that this was but part of the mission that I'd been entrusted with. I've yet to conclude what the other might be."

Upon delving further, Madeleine was able to retrieve two additional volumes. There was still one remaining package to be opened.

"I have absolutely no idea what this could possibly be. Perhaps you should open it, Michel."

Handling the package with a delicacy that belied his muscular strength, Michel found that he was shaking. Like Madeleine, he, too, wondered about its contents.

When the last of the wrapping had been drawn away, he was shocked to discover that it contained the fleur-de-lis cross of his dear, sweet Maman, Geneviève Baillon.

Silent tears spilled over, coursing down his cheeks.

This was the very crucifix that his Papa had presented to Maman, celebrating his birth as their first born, in 1728. She had always vowed never to remove this special piece. For Maman to have passed this special cross along to Mother Pêche was a message that spoke volumes.

Michel held the piece in his sizeable hand, not knowing what else to do.

Madeleine quickly asked him to pass it to her.

Through the use of psychometry, a means of being able to obtain information about an individual through paranormal means (by making physical contact with an object belonging to that person), she was able to assure Michel that his family had not been separated as a result of the deportation.

"Thank you for that reassurance, Madeleine. As difficult as it will be to learn to adjust to your time, this knowing will make it easier for me."

Unbeknownst to Michel, his father, Honoré LeBlanc, had commissioned two identical fleur-de-lis pieces, both to commemorate his descent from King Clovis I.

In retrospect, the gifted piece had belonged to him.

Chapter 8

After much investigation of Madeleine's 10-acre property, Michel discovered some strangely familiar landmarks.

Asking Madeleine why she had purchased this particular property, she merely shrugged her shoulders, saying that she'd been strongly drawn to the house, and the property, well in advance of her time travel experience.

He shared with her what he had come to believe; that this property had previously belonged to Madame Pêche.

"But Michel, how could this be the same property that Madame lived on? She lived in the village of Grand Pré. We are living in Gaspereau."

"What you need to understand is that the area known as Grand Pré took in a much larger area, in my time, than that which you today call Grand Pré. I assure you, this *is* the very property."

“But when she found me at Saint-Charles-des-Mines we walked but a few miles to the homestead. There is no way that we could have covered this distance.”

“With the amount of adrenaline that must have been pumping through your body, I doubt very much that you paid attention to the length of time it took you to walk from the church.”

Madeleine’s shoulders slumped dejectedly.

“You may be right. I don’t know. It’s strange. Now that I am back, everything just seems so hazy.”

Michel continued to explore, discovering the remnants of an old building, long overgrown, covered with brush and weeds.

Proceeding to dig, he was quick to discover what appeared to be the outline of a home, complete with a root cellar that seemed to branch off into what looked, passably, like a tunnel of sorts, but he could not be sure.

All had fallen in and would not be safe to investigate without the proper equipment.

Feeling a cold shiver pass through his body, he was intuitively drawn to the thought that immediately came to mind, acting on it right away.

Covering the distance, emblazoned firmly in his mind, he uncovered a stone-lined well. Having made his way to that same well countless times, over a period of nine years, Michel shone, downward into the well, the special light that Madeleine had given him.

Sure enough, he could see where the footholds were, just like friends of old.

He positioned the special headlight around his forehead so that the light was projecting downward, towards his feet. Putting the backpack on backwards, across his chest, he tied it securely, from back to front, with a bungie cord.

He knew that he only had to descend five feet into the depths of the well in order to locate what he was after.

Sure enough, there it was.

He had managed to locate what Madame had requested of him.

She had wanted him to loosen several stones in a specific location so that she could hide some small metal boxes when the time came for her to do so.

It was now time to see if he was right.

Removing the loose stones, Michel easily discovered two metal boxes. In sheer elation, knowing that he had, once again, been able to reconnect with his time, tears began to stream down his face.

More than likely, Madeleine's cousin, Gabriel, had been the one to assist Madame in this particular endeavor.

Having climbed back up and out of the well, Michel took a few moments to take a better look at the metal boxes. Sure enough, etched with names, one saying Michel and the other Madeleine, he now had, in his hands, the definitive proof that he needed.

The corners of each box had been sealed with a waxy substance, more than likely to prevent mildew, knowing, full well, that it would be another 250 years in the future before they would be found.

He hurried home to show Madeleine what he had uncovered.

There was a letter in each box, dually signed as both Madame Pêche as well as Jacques de Molay.

My dearest Madeleine, it is with great feeling and deep emotion that I pen these words to you. I am well pleased with the tenacity that you were able to steadfastly apply during your sojourn with me in the eighteenth century.

It was so comforting to be able to pass my knowledge onto you, a fellow time traveler. Had the same not happened to me, I would never have believed it myself.

I know that you are deeply troubled by my imminent return to France as Jacques de Molay. All I can say is that I am duty bound to my Templar brethren to return as their Grand Master. I shall do what needs to be done, as denoted by the stars at the time of my birth.

Know that everything always works out as it is meant. This is why you are doubly blessed to have been able to return to your time with Michel at your side.

I can now rest with much ease, knowing that you, my dearest godchild, as I explained to you when you were with me in Grand Pré, are where you need to be.

I leave you with several personal items of great import to your mission.

You need to know that the skull was found beneath the temple mount of King Solomon. Up until now, it had been handed down to each successive Grand Master. Knowing that I shall be the last of this line, I am bequeathing it to you.

You shall be the one to uncover its mystery.

Madeleine had been gifted with a skull carved out of Libyan Desert Glass, or LDG, an enigmatic type of natural glass made of fused silica, discovered in 1932 and "located between sand dunes of the southwestern corner of the Great

Sand Sea in western Egypt, near the border to Libya."[12] Like Moldavite, LDG is classified as a tektite, meaning that it is of meteoric material.

Most tektites are black, aside from Moldavite, which ranges from pale to dark apple green. By comparison, LDG specimens can range anywhere from a gorgeous straw yellow to a pale, apple green. They often contain small dark speckles, which are remnants of meteor dust.

Madeleine would later come to learn that scientists were claiming this glass to be at least 30 million years old.

Madeleine would also discover that a carved scarab, found in the center of a breastplate located in the KV62 burial chamber belonging to King Tutankhamen, better known as King Tut, had been crafted from this same glass.

Why would she have gifted me with this piece?

---

[12] http://www.lpi.usra.edu/meetings/largeimpacts2003/pdf/4079.pdf accessed on December 24, 2008

Clearly, Madeleine was meant to conduct further research into the noted affiliation between the Templar Knights, secret societies, mystery schools and skulls.

Having previously read The Secret in the Bible by Tony Bushby, there was a hidden message that she had to piece together, one word per chapter, in order to string them all together.

The message, in question, *Learn deeply of the mind and its mystery for therein lies the true secret of immortality*, was a sixteen word sentence that had been "extracted from the ancient *Book of God*, a mysterious old document written on fabric of an unknown nature, and highly regarded by the Ancients thousands of years ago." [13]

On an intuitive level, she knew that this was where she had to place her focus, especially if she were to determine why Madame had gifted her with the skull.

---

[13] Bushby, Tony (2003). *The Secret in The Bible* (p 6). Queensland, AU: Joshua Books.

To Madeleine, she'd also bequeathed a Templar cross pendant, crafted from gold; inscribed on the back was the name *Jacques de Molay*.

A pouch containing a handful of French coins minted in La Rochelle in 1305, several years before he and his Templar brothers would have been arrested, at dawn, under orders of King Philip IV on that fateful day of October 13, 1307, had also been placed in the metal box.

The final piece was a set of rosary beads, crafted in a combination of Baltic Amber and Jet, that looked as if they could easily be draped over the neck, worn as both [1] a purifier of negative energies from one's aura and [2] a protector against negative influences and malicious energies, as well as [3] a facilitator of health and wellness, drawing out infections and cleansing contaminants from bodily organs.

Both stones, if indeed they could be called stones, were said to be able to absorb negativity, processing it into clear, usable energy.

This triggered Madeleine to remember, in the course of her Crystal Healing Practitioner studies, what she'd learned about Wilhelm Reich and his orgone energy accumulator.

It was in November of 1957 that "a world famous physician and scientist died in a U.S. federal penitentiary where he had been imprisoned for resisting an unlawful injunction designed to stop his vital research, steal his discoveries, and kill the discovery." [14] This was later proven to be "the culmination of more than 10 years of harassment and persecution at the hands of carefully concealed conspirators who used U.S. Federal Agencies and Courts to defraud the people of this earth and prevent them from knowing and utilizing crucial discoveries in physics, medicine, and sociology which could help bring about the happiness and peace for all mankind." [15] Madeleine was intuitive enough to know that things would soon be changing.

Orgone energy, Madeleine had learned, was an *inexpensive* way to help restore balance to the Earth.

---

[14] Bernard, Raymond (1969). *The Hollow Earth* (p 8). Secaucus, NJ: Citadel Press for University Books Inc.
[15] Ibid.

Orgonite is an orgone energy transformer as well as an energy generator. Made of cured fiberglass resin, metal chips, copper coils and crystals, they have the ability to capture orgone energy and reverse its negative polarity, healing all living things within its vicinity. Used by practitioners of Geomancy and Feng Shui, these devices have long been used for correcting energy imbalances.

In short, this simple, yet subtle technology, unknown by a great many, has the ability to improve the energetic quality of our environment.

Knowing that both the Baltic Amber (fossilized tree resin that has been appreciated for its beauty since Neolithic times) and Jet (fossilized wood, from millions of years ago, that decomposed under extreme pressure) were privy to ancient Earth Wisdom, Madeleine was quick to reflect on another favorite crystal – Iolite.

Given her keen interest in crystals and minerals, Madeleine had learned that Iolite could be used "as an aid for those attempting to access information from past lives, having a special attunement to the periods of history associated with the Cathars, the Knights Templar and the Arthurian Legends." [16]

It had also been shared that Iolite could be used for "opening the portals of memory so one can learn and integrate the appropriate past-life lessons to assist in one's current incarnation." [17]

Likewise, the ancient mariners (Vikings), using the strong pleochroism of this stone, were able to look through thin Iolite lenses (thin slices of the stone) in order to determine the exact position of the sun on overcast days, thereby navigating their way safely to the New World and back again. In its day, it could have been referred to as a compass of sorts.

This might certainly explain why she had long been drawn to this particular stone, always carrying it upon her person.

---

[16] Simmons, Robert and Ahsian, Naisha (2005). *The Book of Stones: Who They Are and What They Teach* (p 199). East Montpelier, VT: Heaven and Earth Publishing LLC.
[17] Ibid.

My dearest Michel, it is in having found this box that I know you have made it to the twenty-first century with Madeleine. It was for this reason that I was so diligent in instructing you in the English language. At the time, I was not able to disclose the nature of my instruction to you.

I am well pleased with your tutelage. You shall do very well with Madeleine by your side. You will uncover many a mystery in your time there.

Always remember to trust your heart.

To Michel, she had bequeathed the Knights Templar Grand Master ring, crafted from gold and etched with the seal of the two knights on one horse, the same seal that his forebearer, Bertrand de Blanchefort, a key Grand Master from 1156 to 1169, had been responsible for designing.

Upon further inspection of the ring, Michel discovered the name *Jacques de Molay* etched on the inside of the band.

In addition, there was a second pouch containing a handful of French coins minted in La Rochelle in 1305.

"So you *were* right, Michel, when you claimed that this property was familiar, that Madame had lived here. I guess that would explain why, on a gut level, I knew that I had to purchase this piece of property a little over a year ago, almost a foretelling, of sorts, if you will. Aside from personal experience, this is something that no one else would ever believe."

Knowing that they were holding onto an amazing fortune, Madeleine conveyed the following.

"There is only one person that I can think of to make contact with and that would be archaeologist Jackson Ferguson at Saint Mary's University in Halifax. It was during the summer of 2000 that Jackson and geophysicist Darcy McDonald made use of the Em-38b, an electromagnetic geophysical instrument, one created by Geonics, [18] enabling them to see beneath the ground. That's when they discovered that the well manicured lawn at the Grand-Pré

---

[18] http://www.geonics.com

National Historic Site concealed numerous hidden archaeological sites. [19]

"You see, it was this very work that led to the creation of the Grand-Pré Archaeological Field School Project in 2001, a partnership between the Société Promotion Grand-Pré, Parks Canada and Saint Mary's University in Halifax. They have been working steadily, each summer, since that time."

Michel noticed a smile on Madeleine's face.

"I guess it is not too hard to tell that I was also interested in Archaeology, before I decided to enter into Education. I'll do my best to try and make contact with him over the next couple of days. Would you mind if I invited him out here to take a look at what you've uncovered?"

Michel solemnly shook his head.

"No, I would not mind at all. I, too, am beginning to think that he may well be our best bet."

---

[19] Société Promotion Grand-Pré. *Archaeology: Virtual Excavation* accessed on December 22, 2008 at http://www.grand-pre.com/GrandPreSiteDevelopment/en/Site.html

Chapter 9

It was exciting to speak with Jackson, after so long a time. Madeleine was completely energized at the prospect of an archaeological dig on the property.

Although Jackson had his own team members, she'd somehow managed to convince him that she should be directly involved with the dig; likewise for Michel.

After all, in truth, it was a family affair then, as well as now, although she'd never disclose that pertinent piece of information.

"He's probably going to come by some day next week to take a look around the property. If he feels there's anything worth exploring, he'll be back in the late spring to try and get a dig organized."

Madeleine smiled.

"All we can do now is wait to hear what he has to say.

"I will say this about Jackson, however. He is quite renowned for his expertise when it comes to digs throughout Atlantic Canada. Without giving too much away, perhaps we can drop a few hints as to the nature of the items that we found buried on the property.

"I'm sure that he'll direct us to someone who is schooled in the field of ancient antiquities. I guess you could say that I trust Jackson's judgment, implicitly."

As it turned out, not only did Jackson think that the site was worth exploring, but he was also able to direct Madeleine and Michel to a Jacques Dumont.

Having known JD, as he continually called him, for over twenty years since they were both freshmen at SMU, Jackson shared that he was an expert in the field of dating ancient artifacts, preferring to work with rare pieces of antiquity.

With an ability to date and authenticate anything, Jackson had been inviting him along on the yearly digs at Grand Pré.

While all of this was well and good, it was the knowing that JD had always been interested in things of an arcane and mystical nature that truly gave Madeleine the shivers.

In fact, she just kept getting goosebumps on top of goosebumps on top of goosebumps, an experience that is known as resonating.

This always meant that she'd come into contact with something that she was able to acknowledge as being part of her individual truth.

Until she and Michel actually came face to face with this JD, Madeleine would have no idea how, or why, he was even associated.

That having been said, she knew there to be some type of synchronistic connection with this Jacques Dumont.

Within the week, Madeleine and Michel were traveling to Halifax to meet with JD. He'd asked them to bring their treasures along with them.

While they were a tad uneasy about revealing what Michel had found, they knew that they had to speak with someone who was an expert in this field.

Unbeknownst to Madeleine and Michel, this was to be the start of another grand adventure.

Chapter 10

The morning they were to travel to Halifax, Madeleine found her mind totally preoccupied. While she was more than eager to meet JD, she was also feeling apprehensive, not liking that feeling at all.

How were they going to go about unveiling the nature of their findings, without looking as if they were mad? Aside from divulging information to Kate, this was to be their first foray amongst the populace of the twenty-first century.

Since waking at the break of dawn, Madeleine had been unable to stop thinking about Mother Pêche.

Aside from missing the closest friend she had ever had, both time travelers at a juncture outside of their current realities, she was not sure what she should be feeling.

Madeleine wondered why Mother was such a prominent feature on this particular morning.

Knowing that she had been attempting to connect with the Libyan Desert Glass crystal skull, she was quick to dismiss her feelings as mere synchronicity, forgetting that Mother had always insisted that she learn to fine tune these intuitive glimpses of hers.

Rock formations and crystals are among the oldest structures on this planet.

What continued to make this absolutely fascinating for Madeleine was the fact that there are technology pieces that can actually date geological specimens. In fact, the very history of the planet continues to be referenced through rock formations.

In the course of conducting research on the internet, Madeleine remembered reading about the Dropa disks [20] that were uncovered from a remote mountain cave, near the Himalayan mountain range of Baian-Kara-Ula, by archaeologist Chi Pu Tei in 1938.

---

[20] http://paranormal.about.com/od/ancientanomalies/a/aa060198.htm

These disks appear to tell a story of a space probe by the inhabitants of another planet some 12,000 years ago.

With a total of 716 uncovered disks (along with the skeletons of a pygmy-like people, averaging a little over four feet high), all contained tiny, microscopic characters in an unknown language.

It was in 1962 that Professor Tsum Un Nui, of the Peking Academy of Prehistory, painstakingly transcribed the characters from each disk to paper. The writing was so small that he had to make use of a magnifying glass to see it clearly.

While much of the hieroglyphic language was either too difficult to make out, or had been worn away by elements and time, eventually, however, one word emerged, followed by another.

A phrase that made sense seemed to evolve, followed by an entire sentence. That was when Dr. Nui knew that he had been successful in breaking the code.

When the translation was complete, he could only reflect on the message in sheer disbelief. The Peking Academy of Prehistory, however, forbade him to publish his findings.

Several years later, however, Dr. Nui's findings were published in a paper called *The Grooved Script Concerning Spaceships which, as Recorded on the Discs, Landed on Earth 12,000 Years Ago*. Unfortunately, both his translation as well as his theory was met with ridicule within the archaeological establishment.

In 1968, a Russian scientist conducted tests on the discs that revealed some very peculiar properties. When tested with an oscillograph (a device for recording the wave-forms of changing currents, voltages, or any other quantity that can be translated into electric energy, such as sound waves), a surprising oscillation rhythm was recorded.

It was almost as if they had once been electrically charged and/or had functioned as electrical conductors. In addition, these discs were comprised of cobalt, iron and nickel, the only metals capable of producing a magnetic field.

It was clear that these discs had a very special use.

The whole issue pertaining to crystals comes down to their piezoelectrical ability as being the key factor in all computer transmissions and transactions. It has also been stated that crystals have the capacity to receive, store and transmit large amounts of data.

In and around the same time that the Dropa discs were discovered, archaeologists were finding crystal skulls, a number of which were Mayan skulls, speculated to have been linked to one of thirteen original master skulls.

The oldest storage device on this planet is crystal. Madeleine had been instructed, courtesy of her Crystal Healing Practitioner diploma course, that crystal has memory which, when carved into a skull shape, becomes very focused.

Representative of the higher mind, the skull symbolizes wisdom. The ancients, in fact, were of the belief that the skull was said to house the soul.

Likewise, skulls have been denoted as being messengers of spirituality, knowledge and understanding.

Since Madame, also known as Jacques de Molay, had gifted her with a special skull, Madeleine was quite eager to learn more.

Knowing that crystals are amplifiers and generators of energy, could it be that crystal skulls might act as a satellite dish of sorts, connecting one with the divine, she wondered?

While she personally knew crystals to have a healing effect on the body, she felt this hypothesis might be something that merited further research.

Madeleine had learned that there are three types of crystal skulls; namely, [1] new or contemporary (meaning that they are manufactured by modern carvers), [2] old (having been crafted anywhere from 100 to 1000 years ago) and [3] ancient (ranging anywhere from 1500 to 2000 years of age).

Based on this knowledge, Madeleine knew that her Libyan Desert Glass skull was a rarity piece.

Having named the skull *Inner Glow*, this was the only piece that was housed outside of the metal box in which it had been found. All of the other treasures had been preserved in high resolution digital format; likewise for the volumes that Gabriel had presented to Madeleine on August 2, 1755 (all of which had only ever been touched when wearing latex gloves).

Knowing that the treasures had to be secured in a safe place until they could be assessed, Scotiabank employees had accorded them the privacy they had asked for.

Each item was carefully placed in a single security deposit box. Not wanting to take the treasures on this trip, they decided, against JD's recommendations, setting off for Halifax with digital photos in hand.

Upon entering the Centennial Building on Hollis Street and taking the elevator up to the designated floor, it was there that Madeleine and Michel were met by Ms. Mallet, JD's personal secretary.

They were told, since he would be along shortly, they could make themselves comfortable in his office.

Mere moments later, a rather distinguished gentleman, with slate blue eyes and a dark-skinned, almost swarthy, complexion, entered. His hair was as dark as his face. Greying at the temples, it was pulled back in a ponytail.

There was something mesmerizing, and yet strangely familiar, about those eyes. Once again, Madeleine's mind returned to Mother Pêche. Yes, it was Mother who had had these same eyes. *How strange*, she mused.

Madeleine looked at him again. That could certainly explain why she was experiencing a déjà-vu type feeling.

Smiling, she shook the hand that he proffered. Within a flash, what she experienced was not your typical handshake.

Entering into a trance-like state, Madeleine was overcome with images that seared into her brain.

… the arrest of Jacques de Molay on March 13, 1307 at the hands of King Philippe IV.

… the hideous torture used in order to force him into making false confessions.

… time spent in a dark, dank dungeon.

… the smell of burning flesh being roasted over a fire on an island in the Seine river, in front of the Cathedral Notre Dame de Paris, on March 18, 1314.

Madeleine was also able to hear, with total clarity, his final address to the crowd.

"It is just that, in so terrible a day, and in the last moments of my life, I should discover all the iniquity of falsehood, and make the truth triumph. I declare, then, in the face of heaven and earth, and acknowledge, though to my eternal shame, that I have committed the greatest crimes but it has been the acknowledging of those which have been so foully charged on the order. I attest, and truth obliges me to attest, that it is innocent. I made the contrary declaration only to suspend the excessive pains of torture, and to mollify those who made me endure them. I know the punishments which have been inflicted on all the knights who had the courage to revoke a similar confession; but the dreadful spectacle which is presented to me is not able to make me confirm one lie by another. The life offered me on such infamous terms, I abandon without regret. Let evil swiftly befall those who have wrongly condemned us. God will avenge us." [21]

Knowing the history surrounding this happenstance, Madeleine was aware of the chilling irony of those very words because it was within the year that both King Philippe IV and Pope Clement V had succumbed to death.

Overcome with the sensations that lasted mere seconds, but felt otherwise, Madeleine quickly removed her hand, trying to regain a sense of composure.

"I'm sorry, but I have to sit down."

Michel, very concerned, directed her to the nearest leather chair. He quickly positioned himself in the adjacent chair as JD moved to seat himself behind the desk. He, too, looked rather concerned.

---

[21] *The Story of Jacques DeMolay* website accessed on July 13, 2009 at http://www.jacquesdemolay.org/

Madeleine continued to stare at JD, as if in complete disbelief.

“I don’t believe it. You are here? Why? How? I *really* don’t understand this, you know. I feel as if I’ve just been on the roller coaster ride of my life, and it’s not a ride that I ever care to repeat, thank you very much.”

Michel looked on in alarm, thinking that something had finally sent Madeleine over the edge.

Every day was continuing to be an adjustment for him, as well. He would never be able to explain this quantum journey to anyone, for they would surely lock him up and throw away the key.

JD looked at Michel, but directed his words to Madeleine.

“Before we can continue any further, Madeleine, maybe you need to share, with both of us, what you just experienced.”

Madeleine laughed at JD’s choice of words, knowing that he knew, full well, what had been revealed to her.

She turned to Michel with a look of joy on her face. The first thought entertained by Michel was that he was right; *all of this has just been too much for her*.

Turning to face JD, he stood up and extended his hand, saying, “We are so very sorry to have troubled you, Mr. Dumont.”

Madeleine quickly sent him a look that said *trust me, everything is alright*.

In looking at Madeleine and then JD, both were smiling broadly.

The dark hairs on his forearms, immediately stood upright and at complete attention; the physical confirmation of knowing that something otherworldly had, once again, transpired.

Finding his seat slowly, it was now Michel who felt as if he had just fallen down the rabbit hole, instead of Alice.

Madeleine looked at Michel.

"I know that you have just acknowledged, in your own way, that something of significance has just transpired, and you are quite right. You see, JD is none other than Mother Pêche; it is no wonder, therefore, that she came to my mind first thing this morning."

Michel slowly turned to face JD, who quickly acquiesced by giving a slight affirmative nod of his head.

"As I was shaking his hand, I experienced many visions, simultaneously, all of which were connected with Jacques de Molay."

Looking directly at JD, she posed the question.

"Tell me that I haven't lost my mind. You truly are Jacques de Molay, the last Grand Master of the Knights Templar, aka Madame Pêche, are you not?"

"Correction, my dear Madeleine, I *was* Jacques de Molay, yes."

At that very instant, someone else entered the room in a flurry.

Madeleine immediately became transfixed on the individual, not because he was clearly of aboriginal ancestry, but because he reminded her so much of Gabriel Sinclair.

Of a similar height, he, too, had long, straight, blue-black hair, plaited into a solitary braid that fell to the middle of his back.

Introduced as Gavin Stewart, business partner to JD, the newcomer walked towards Madeleine, hand proffered for the customary handshake.

Once again, and as quickly as before, she experienced a déjà-vu of monumental proportions. Before she was able to release her hand, tears began to quickly stream down her face.

As fast as she endeavored to wipe them away, they were immediately replaced anew.

It was the space of several moments before Madeleine was able to fully compose herself.

"I should have known that where I would find one, I would also find the other. I am so happy to be with you again, my cousin."

Turning to face a twice-stunned Michel, she was quick to explain.

"I know that this is too much to take in, especially after meeting JD, but Gavin is actually Gabriel Sinclair, my Mi'kmaq cousin of your time."

Madeleine turned back to Gavin, who had since seated himself in the third leather chair in front of the desk, with a beaming smile.

"You knew that we would cross paths after our return to my time, so quick were you to reassure me, then, that we would meet again.

"Clearly, we were destined to meet during the time just prior to the deportation. To have connected once again, and so quickly at that, has thrown me for a loop."

Madeleine sat down, unsure what to say next.

“Indeed, you have intuited correctly, *ma petite*. The four of us are part of something much bigger than even I can adequately share at this time.”

“Which can only be connected to the Aramaic codex as written by Yeshua,” Madeleine deduced further.

“Speaking of which, JD, what can we legally do with the rare treasures that you so brilliantly left for us to find on my Gaspereau property? Also, how do we go about acquiring the necessary documents for Michel?”

“Let me ponder these questions over the course of the next few days. In the meantime, today has clearly proven to be the whirlwind of a day that both Gavin and I’d been anticipating, hasn’t it?”

Madeleine nodded with a heavy head.

“With the adrenaline rushes experienced today, I feel so very tired. A strong coffee from Tim Horton’s is *definitely* in order.”

With a tired smile, she also added, "You know what has been so priceless about today? The very fact that Michel and I didn't even need to bring along our digital photos. That is the part that has been an absolute hoot."

JD smiled, most knowingly.

"Until we'd met face to face, I was not at liberty to say *Oh, and by the way Madeleine, you do not need to bother showing me your treasures because Gavin and I are fully aware of them*, now could I?"

With each of them sipping a Tim Horton's coffee, Madeleine and Michel were soon heading back to their home in the Annapolis Valley.

Chapter 11

For Madeleine, the remainder of the week passed as if she were waking up from a fantastic dream.

The fact that Jacques Dumont (aka Madame Pêche, aka Jacques de Molay), Gavin Stewart (aka Gabriel Sinclair) and Michel were all here together, with her, was ample proof that each of them had their own role to play in the completion of that which had long been foretold.

It was an honorary destiny to be a collective part of what was to come.

"So what is the secret to living in the here and now?" Madeleine queried.

"The same that it's always been, *ma petite*," Gavin answered. "The purpose of life is a truly wondrous thing. We're here to experience joy. We're here to experience appreciation. We're here to experience passion. We're here to experience the freedom of choosing our own thoughts.

"In this physical body, all are an extension of what we call God. In keeping with individual expansion, we're here to both experience and observe, for it's in the knowing what we don't want that we are able to reach for what we do want. Following me, so far?"

Madeleine gave a quick nod so that Gavin could continue.

"With regards to everything that exists, you already know that thought has always come first. This means, quite simply, that everything you see around you was once a thought or an idea. In fact, everything was a vibrational concept before manifesting in physical reality.

"You see, this entire process is all about aligning your thoughts with feelings of joy, appreciation, passion, excitement, enthusiasm and expansion, as these feelings are specific to the spiritual beings that we are. When you have achieved this vibrational alignment, this vibrational harmony, with the inner you, any action that you feel inspired to take will feel absolutely marvelous.

"Your true work is to realign with your innate essence, the spiritual being having the physical experience, for it is only then that you allow creation (manifestation) to take place."

"What you are saying, Gavin, is that "it's not action that matters; it's your vibration. It's not what you are doing that makes the difference; it's how you are feeling about what you are doing,"[22] correct?

"Of course, this also means that if I'm not feeling good about something, then I'm not in alignment with who I really am. This means that before I can affect the change that I desire, I must take the necessary steps to make myself *feel* better."

"By Jove, I think she's summed it up rather nicely. But don't forget that "whatever is most active in your vibration is what will continue to occur in your experience."[23] This is what many, today, refer to as the Law of Attraction.

---

[22] Hicks, Esther and Jerry. (2007) *The Astonishing Power of Emotions: Let Your Feelings Be Your Guide* (p 61). Carlsbad, CA: Hay House, Inc.
[23] Ibid, p. 92.

"By caring about the way you feel, regardless of the circumstances in which you find yourself, one can live a joyous experience. You are the *only* being who can affect that change, whatever it may be. Your happiness, or not, is dependent solely on you. In finding thoughts that are pleasing to you, in placing your trust in the universe, you shall receive wondrous opportunities and experiences, all of which will continue to serve you in your ever-growing enthusiasm and expansion."

Madeleine nodded in total agreement, before commenting.

"When it comes to visualization, I find it incredibly difficult to see the pictures and try to put myself in the image. It's really hard for me to get emotionally excited when all my mind sees are some dark and fuzzy attempts at a new reality.

"Being the avid researcher and questioner that you know me to be, sometime ago I discovered Mind Movies, [24] an absolutely phenomenal metaphysical tool.

---

[24] http://www.mindmovies.com/?10107

"I have since discovered that it really doesn't matter if you can't visualize very well, as long as you know how to watch videos. Likewise, it really doesn't matter if you can't raise your emotional vibration easily, as long as you like music."

Gavin continued to look at Madeleine in a blank, unseeing, sort of way.

"Let me tell you more. Mind Movies is a multi-media tool that allows you to create a vision, a picture, of what you want, scored with your favorite song; the one that makes you feel good, the one that makes you want to dance, the one that makes you smile and sing along. It becomes this very process that allows you to make your dreams and desires a monumental part of what you see and hear every day because it is all related to the *feeling* that you keep talking about.

"When you watch your Mind Movie every morning and every evening, you are actually assisting the manifestation process, all courtesy of the Law of Attraction."

The excitement and enthusiasm that Madeleine was spreading was becoming infectious. She even giggled.

“I know, I know, I guess I’m going to have to show you the Mind Movie that I made before my discovering 1754 Acadie. I just didn’t expect to get catapulted back in time to find what I’d been searching for.”

Gavin interjected. “The universe has its own way of delivering what it is that we are creating, of that there can be no doubt.”

“Having been privy to this on a regular basis, I definitely concur with you on this point, Gavin.”

Madeleine laughed delightedly, knowing that everything was coming together.

Chapter 12

Given that Madeleine was the rightful owner of the property upon which the treasures were discovered, albeit some 250 years after the fact, JD informed them that the artifacts rightly belonged to them.

They could, if they wanted, make a donation, of sorts, to the National Historic Park at Grand Pré.

Knowing the Templar history behind several pieces, namely, the cross, crafted from gold, and the ring, both belonging to the last Grand Master, these could never be shared with anyone. Madeleine and Michel rightly felt that they belonged with JD.

Passing them back to the very individual who had managed to keep them safely hidden for the sake of future posterity, was an emotional experience for all; a re-acquaintance with old friends.

The gold coins, minted in La Rochelle in 1305, alluded to the fact that men had traveled to these very shores, even prior to the voyage of Henry Sinclair.

In keeping with the Baltic Amber and Jet rosary beads, Madeleine was quite eager to share this find with others, thereby allowing them to become part of the encased display at Grand Pré.

Given her metaphysical background, she also included a piece that she had composed, basically in reference to their metaphysical properties (refer back to page 93 for the particulars).

It was a big relief when JD, true to his word, and without sharing how he'd managed to accomplish it, also came through with the necessary documents for Michel.

As an antiquities dealer, JD had also been informed of a remarkable piece: the twin to the fleur-de-lis cross as commissioned by Michel's father, Honoré LeBlanc, in 1728.

The cross had been a family heirloom for as long as anyone could remember.

JD had successfully put Michel in touch with one of his modern-day cousins, a woman named Sophie, and she was able to tell him what she knew about it.

Words are not adequate to describe that momentous day. Many tears were shed as cousins came to meet cousins.

Over the course of many conversations, Michel came to learn that his fleur-de-lis cross had belonged to his dear Papa.

The piece that had belonged to his dear Maman, then, had been gifted to the oldest daughter, none other than Michel's sister, Sophie, nine years younger than he.

In turn, thereafter, it had been passed down from mother to oldest daughter, always named Sophie, therein begetting the family tradition.

Just as Michel hadn't known of the second matching piece, so, too, was it the same for his sister's family.

It was through the course of this remarkable discovery that Michel was finally able to re-connect with family.

Michel also learned that his own immediate family had been shipped to Pennsylvania, aboard the Hannah, leaving Grand Pré on October 27, 1755, and arriving on November 19, 1755. [25] Both a sloop as well as a schooner, these were the primary vessels used in transporting the Acadian people.

Given their most unexpected arrival, the Acadians had to remain in port for several months, living on a diet of pork and flour, while also in dire need of blankets, shirts, stockings and other necessities. [26] Disease soon spread rampant amongst the ships that were quarantined in the Delaware harbor, killing close to half of the Acadian population, it is said, as well as Michel's dear Maman.

Although Pennsylvania was founded by Quakers seeking religious tolerance, they shunned the French Catholic Acadians that turned up on their shores. Bordered on the west by French territory, they were probably quite frightened at the prospect of a possible French invasion.

---

[25] http://www.landrystuff.com/ExpulsionShips.html
[26] http://www.acadian-home.org/PennsylvaniaExiles-Ledet.html

By March 5, 1756, some three months later, the Acadians were dispersed throughout the colony. [27]

By January 18, 1757, the Governor approved the binding out of Acadian boys and girls, under the age of twenty-one, as apprentices, whereby they would both learn a trade as well as the English language, [28] even though the government was fairly lax in enforcing this law.

Clearly, the Acadians knew naught if they were subjects, prisoners, slaves or freemen, [29] a sad state of affairs.

In general, the Acadians did not fare well in Pennsylvania.

At the time of their arrival, the physical condition of many was rather miserable. Many months spent aboard crowded, and disease-infested ships, served to create an even more deplorable situation.

---

[27] http://www.acadian-cajun.com/expa.htm
[28] Ibid.
[29] http://www.acadian-home.org/PennsylvaniaExiles-Ledet.html

They were ill-clothed and undernourished, making them even more susceptible to disease. In truth, it was smallpox that decimated many of them.

From the time of their arrival in 1755, until the year 1766, about ten thousand pounds were paid, out of the provincial treasury, for the relief of the Acadian people. [30]

Between 1766 and 1767, there were at least one hundred fifty, and perhaps as many as two hundred, Pennsylvania Acadians, who left for Louisiana. [31]

As a result of the fleur-de-lis cross discovery, it was JD who'd successfully located Michel's family in Louisiana, a feat that Michel would never forget.

---

[30] http://www.acadian-home.org/PennsylvaniaExiles-Ledet.html
[31] http://www.acadian-cajun.com/expa.htm

Chapter 13

Now that they were all back together again, JD, Gavin, Michel and Madeleine, there was a motto that kept reverberating over and over again in Madeleine's head – *All for One, and One for All.*

Indeed, the motto was quite apt, for this was exactly how she felt. Perhaps they were to become knights of their own modern-day round table.

Madeleine had always been drawn to the premise upon which Camelot was said to have been built. Here, everyone, from the noble man down to the common man, had rights.

Women were respected and not used.

A man's word was his bond.

Chivalry existed in the form of courtesy, generosity, valor, courage, honor, justice, universal love, nobility, purity of heart, and a readiness to help the weak; a form of living love and personal code of conduct, if you will.

People fought for what they believed in, as opposed to being forced to fight against their will by an overlord.

After all, was it not more important to fight with ideas and compassion, with forbearance and brilliantly conceived non-violent strategies, as well as with tolerance? [32]

Does not the same hold true now?

Are not these the laws of life?

When one added the Holy Grail to the mix, well, it just became even more exciting, depending, of course, on your definition of the Holy Grail.

While it may or may not have existed in reality, Madeleine had always believed Camelot to be a state of mind. In truth, Camelot accords us a glimpse of what humankind can aspire to upon recognizing their connection, their oneness, to God/dess.

---

[32] Hearth, William. (2008) *Ormus: The Secret Alchemy of Mary Magdalene Revealed – Part A: Historical and Practical Applications of Essential Alchemical Science* (p. 4). Delaware, NJ: Ormus Publications and Booksellers LLC.

Sir Thomas More wrote *Utopia* in 1516. Likewise, Sir Frances Bacon published *The New Atlantis*, a Utopian novel, in English in 1627; a work that depicted generosity and enlightenment, dignity and splendor, piety and public spirit, as commonly held qualities of importance. [33]

It also needed to be remembered that the 1398 pre-Columbian voyage of Henry Sinclair, to the New World, to Acadie, was also an attempt to establish an idyllic safe haven for both Grail refugees (a direct female descendant of the Elchasai line, courtesy of Miriam of Bethany, as well as a direct female descendant connected with the Æthiopian connection, courtesy of Mirium Magdalene, known to us as Mary Magdalene) as well as French Templar knights.

Can it not be said, then, that Yeshua was part of this same perceptive intelligence that we have long come to associate with Camelot?

In alchemical terms, it was the *squaring of the circle* that represented "the coming together of male and female

---

[33] http://en.wikipedia.org/wiki/New_Atlantis

elements in perfect harmony and dimension," [34] which was another way of talking about the complete balancing of both aspects of one's self; namely, the Yin (masculine) and the Yang (feminine).

Having mastered such a formula, one would then have completed the alchemical change of taking lead (one's ego-based existence) and turning it into gold (a heart-based consciousness); in essence, the perfecting of humankind, the making of man as God; the true philosopher's stone, if you will.

Given their tentative alliances with both the Arabs and the Jews, we know that the Knights Templar would "have been party to all types of learning and thought." [35]

Might both the church and state, then, have envied, not only the riches of the Templars, but their vast knowledge (power) as well?

---

[34] Mann, William F. (2004). *The Knights Templar in the New World: How Henry Sinclair Brought the Grail to Acadia* (p. 28). Rochester, VT: Destiny Books.
[35] Ibid, p 32.

Clearly, they had discovered something of tremendous religious and historical value; something that may have confirmed the existence of Yeshua, as well as the true nature of spirituality, but clearly in a manner *not* embraced by the church.

It was the belief of the Templars that "the soul lies in the head and not in the heart." [36] In essence, the Templars believed that it was through mental reasoning and logic (the brain) that they could rationalize the very breadth of their soul.

Metaphysically speaking, the symbol of the skull represents the higher mind, meaning that in order to attain the higher mind of spiritual awareness, which also includes psychic ability, we must be released from the thrall of the lower cognitive mind. [37]

---

[36] Mann, William F. (2004). *The Knights Templar in the New World: How Henry Sinclair Brought the Grail to Acadia* (p. 71). Rochester, VT: Destiny Books.
[37] Crystal Skull Head Quarters eBay store located at http://stores.ebay.ca/Crystal-Skull-Head-Quarters

The Templars also knew that their relationship to God/dess was a personal one; hence, here was no need for any intermediary. Likewise, they revered this wisdom, this knowledge, this truth, for theirs was a Gnostic state of mind (inner consciousness).

In the earlier writings, they understood that Yeshua had been portrayed more as a spirit of God than an actual son of God, an awareness to which all can attain.

They knew that love, compassion and kindness were the components that allow the individual to ascend to a higher plane, a higher awareness, a higher level of consciousness.

It may well have been this infinite and absolute knowledge that also contributed to their power.

Chapter 14

When Madeleine and Michel met with their friends Gavin and JD, as was typically the case, Madeleine was the one to begin the conversation.

"You know, I was reading, some time ago, that "the first Acadians had names such as Belliveau, Comeau, Doucet, Dugas, Gallant, LeBlanc, Robichaud, Saulnier, and Mellanson, whose family origins provide a hint that many Acadians, specifically the Mellansons, were, in all probability, descendants of the Holy Family." [38] Not only that, but there is a Doucet Surname Family Tree DNA Project [39] that is showing some most interesting results. What do you make of this?"

"First off, tell us about the DNA findings, in keeping with the Doucet surname," queried JD, "because it might shed more light on the brevity of the conversation."

---

[38] Mann, William F. (2006). *The Templar Meridians: The Secret Mapping of the New World* (p. 233). Rochester, VT: Destiny Books.
[39] http://www.familytreedna.com/public/Doucet/default.aspx

“It is known that Germain Doucet traveled with Commander Isaac de Razilly to re-establish the colony following the Saint Germain-en-Laye Treaty of March 29, 1632. There’s one R1b participant who does not match any of the other R1b results to date. While he may eventually connect back with the other R1b Doucet males, his DNA marker results take him much farther back than the known arrival of Germain Doucet, perhaps by well over 1,000 years.”

Madeleine could see that JD’s slate-blue eyes were alight with mischief.

“You have a fairly good idea what this means, don’t you, JD?”

“Why, yes, I think I have a strong inkling, Madeleine. As well you know, there were thirteen ships that sailed from the Orkney Islands in 1398, all under the care and direction of Henry Sinclair, your ancestor.

“Most of the men sailing with him on this transatlantic voyage were French.

"It appears that both the Grail refugees, and the Knights Templar, pushed inward from their initial Nova Scotia haven. By about 1580, they had reached the Niagara, with further evidence suggesting that "they simply melded into the frontier life of New France." [40] In addition, it was this sort of discovered pattern that also seems to answer "some of the perplexing questions about the Acadians, such as why some Acadian family genealogies are up to ten generations too long to fit in with known colonizations." [41] Do you see where I am going with this information?"

Madeleine nodded her head, slowly and thoughtfully.

"I think so. If we can now fast forward to the time of Champlain and the establishment of Québec City in 1611, it was the intent of both Cardinal Richelieu and Champlain to establish a permanent colony in New France with a population of at least four thousand before 1643. [42]

---

[40] Mann, William F. (2004). *The Knights Templar in the New World: How Henry Sinclair Brought the Grail to Acadia* (p. xiii). Rochester, VT: Destiny Books.
[41] Ibid.
[42] Ibid, p. 111.

"However, the Kirke brothers of England foiled their plans in 1628. At the time of Champlain's death on December 25, 1635, there were but 150 French men and women living in the colony." [43]

It was at this point that Gavin responded.

"I must commend you, *ma petite*, on the astounding knowledge that you possess in reference to French history of the earlier days."

"I've always known more about the French side of my family as opposed to the Scottish, so, yes, I concur with you in that I am rather astonishing in my knowledge base."

Michel laughed heartily before responding.

"While this is true, *ma déesse enchanteresse*, it is I, *ton mari dévot*, who has lived the true experience, as has both Gavin and JD, non?"

---

[43] Mann, William F. (2004). *The Knights Templar in the New World: How Henry Sinclair Brought the Grail to Acadia* (p. 112). Rochester, VT: Destiny Books.

Madeleine stuck her tongue out at him before continuing.

“While that may all be well and good, I still do not understand how those Acadian names figure into this Grail story of ours? Surely someone here can enlighten me.”

JD had held off long enough, knowing how antsy she was.

“In addition to what I shared earlier about the Grail refugees, and the Knights Templar, melding into the frontier life of New France, so, too, did they merge with the Acadian settlements that were established by de Razilly.

“This meant that there were particular Acadian genealogies that contained too many generations to even begin to support the idea that these families had come to Acadia with de Razilly. In fact, there was a documentary made in 1993, by the National Film Board of Canada, called *It's In the Genes*, in reference to the LeBlanc family. [44] So you see, some of

---

[44] Bradley, Michael. (1998) *Grail Knights of North America: On the Trail of the Grail Legacy in Canada and the United States* (pp. 277 to 278). Toronto, ON: Dundurn Press.

these men, and possibly their families, were already in Acadia before the Acadians arrived."

"Another tidbit of information, if I may," added Gavin, with a smile.

"There was a Monseignor Bourgeois of Moncton, New Brunswick, who used to end every sermon with these very words ... *Never forget that we are descendants of the knights and the Apostles.* He died in either 1992 or 1993. [45] I was privileged to be in attendance on several occasions."

Then it was back to JD.

"What we also need to remember, aside from all of this, is that Henry Sinclair was a "man of medieval Europe, a man of reason and chivalry, born in a world of the Black Death and the Crusades and a rising Church. The true purpose of this man and his fellow Knights Templar, who safeguarded the Holy Bloodline, was nothing less than to establish a New

---

[45] Bradley, Michael. (1998) *Grail Knights of North America: On the Trail of the Grail Legacy in Canada and the United States* (p. 278). Toronto, ON: Dundurn Press.

Jerusalem, to rebuild the city and its Temple, to make a place where all people could live in harmony and be free to recognize God in any chosen form."[46]

Michel agreed.

"Perhaps we all need to re-establish our focus on the purpose of our return to this time; namely, the implication of Yeshua's work."

---

[46] Mann, William F. (2006). *The Templar Meridians: The Secret Mapping of the New World* (p. 287). Rochester, VT: Destiny Books.

Chapter 15

Madeleine hung up the phone, giving a huge sigh of relief.

"Well, I've just heard back from Jackson Ferguson. He and geophysicist Darcy McDonald will be by the first week in May, taking a cursory meander of the property, while also making use of the Em-38b. I've let them know that we both want to be involved, as much as possible, but that it might be a little more difficult for me than for you."

Responding with a puzzled look, Michel waited patiently, knowing that additional information would soon be forthcoming.

"You're not even going to ask me what I meant by the fact that it would be more difficult for me to become involved on the archaeological dig than you?"

Michel knew how cryptic Madeleine could be, and there were times when he was not sure how to respond. This was definitely one of those times.

Exasperated, Madeleine could take no more. She raced to the bedroom for a pillow, returning with it suitably stuffed under her loose shirt.

Smacking himself on the forehead, Michel broke out into a huge grin before picking her up and twirling them both around, making sure to set her down as gingerly as possible.

“You’re pregnant! That’s wonderful. When is the baby due? How are you feeling? Do you need to sit down? Do you need to rest?”

“Whoa … after all of those questions, I definitely need to find a place to sit.”

Leading him by the hand to the sofa, they sat down together.

Taking a deep breath, Madeleine began.

“I bought a home pregnancy test and the results came back positive. I went to see my doctor and she was able to confirm that I might be close to 10 weeks pregnant, but an ultrasound will be much more definitive.”

Madeleine gave him time to digest the information.

“Explain this word … ultrasound?”

“An ultrasound involves exposing parts of the body to high frequency sound waves. These sound waves produce pictures of the inside of the body. In some cases, they can even tell you the sex of the baby.”

“As long as the child is healthy, why would anyone want to know if it were a boy or a girl?”

“You, my caring and considerate, husband, are exactly right. I’ll be needing to have an ultrasound between 18 and 20 weeks, to better determine the due date, but that is still another few months away. All I know is that this baby was conceived in 1755 and will be born in 2006. That is just too far out there, even for me.”

Madeleine giggled.

“The tales we shall have to tell this wee one, will be rather incredulous, won’t they?”

Michel looked at her with a concerned look. “Are you sure that you are going to be able to keep teaching?”

Madeleine was quick to deliver a punch.

“Did your Maman stop working every time she found out that she was pregnant?”

Michel had the grace to look a tad sheepish.

“I’ll continue to teach up until the Easter holidays before taking my maternal leave, and you, my fine husband, will simply have to do your utmost to keep me happy and contented.”

Drawing Madeleine into his embrace, Michel responded with undue authority.

“And there you have it. I will do as you have asked, *ma déesse enchanteresse*. Your wish is my command.”

“I’m feeling a tad sleepy; maybe a wee nap will suffice.”

Entwined in each other’s arms, they drifted off to sleep.

Chapter 16

The following day, JD, Gavin, Michel, Madeleine and Kate met at mid-day for brunch.

After disclosing the news of her pregnancy, to considerable hoopla and significant tears, she stated that she wanted two godfathers, JD and Gavin, naturally, and one godmother, Kate. She even went so far as to suggest that they come up with their own ceremony; end of discussion.

It was agreed that they would begin working on further translations of Yeshua's words within the coming weeks. Both Gavin and Madeleine felt very strongly about the need to create workshops based on this codex of information.

They bristled at the thought of presenting the material as New Age when, in fact, it was ancient mysticism at its best; most probably some of the same material upon which both mystery schools and secret societies had been built.

Knowing that they could leave the authentication and validation process to JD, they wanted to be prepared, well before the information was made public, especially now that Madeleine was pregnant.

Their aim was to have everything completed and ready to go after Jackson and Darcy had completed their excavation of Madeleine's property, which could, quite conceivably, be within five to six months following the birth.

While it seemed as if they had lots of time, a little over a year in fact, it also had to be remembered that Madeleine was still teaching, meaning that the bulk of the work was going to have to be completed by her three amigos.

She'd simply have to do her best to remain on the sidelines, aside from vacation time, listening to their conversations and editing wherever necessary.

Chapter 17

What follows herein are mere snippets, as taken from the translated message of Yeshua, interspersed with comments by Madeleine.

The message from Yeshua, in its entirety, can be located in the prequel, *A Travel in Time to Grand Pré*.

We are a melding of *God-man* (the mind of God expressing in human form) and *man-God* (physical man expressing the God within), a combined merger of spiritual and physical that serves to continue the expansion of the Father into forever.

A most apt descriptor of a spiritual being engaged within a physical experience; a fact that is being denoted by many of today's spiritual authors and writers

Could this not also have been what the Cathars were trying to express in summation of their beliefs about Yeshua?

During the early formation of what would later come to be known as Christianity, church authorities (deemed Fathers of the Church of Rome) exerted considerable influence (energy) in weeding out what they termed *false* doctrine.

The Cathars (stated to have been derived from the Greek word, *katharoi*, meaning pure ones), it is said, most emulated the Gnostics.

While the writings of the Cathars have, for the most part, been destroyed (because of the doctrinal threat as perceived by the Papacy), there are a few texts that were preserved by their opponents.

The *Rituel Cathare de Lyon* provides us with a mere glimpse of the inner workings of their faith.

A Latin manuscript, *The Book of Two Principles*, kept in Florence, is "a translation made in 1260 from a work by the Cathar Jean de Lugio from Bergamo (written in 1230). The Latin translation, found in Prague in 1939, came from an anonymous treaty written in Languedoc at the beginning of the 13th century." [47] It is conceivable that the author may have been the Parfait Barthelemy of Carcassonne. This particular work outlines "the basis of a complete dualism that is reflected in a veiled way in the Holy Scriptures." [48]

In accordance with Cathari belief, Jesus came to transmit a message, to reveal the truth (as related to our real eternal and spiritual essence) and not to redeem the sins of all men by his death.

Likewise, the beliefs of the Cathars very much coincided with Jesus' example of life (through his teachings): "non-violence but pure love, rejection of using evil or force to resist the evil, and holy will in responding to attacks of the evil only with sacrifice." [49]

Their message was one of love, tolerance, freedom and equality between men and women.

---

[47] The Books by Gilles C. H.Nullens accessed on April 25, 2011 at http://www.nullens.org/catholics-heretics-and-heresy/part-1-the-cathars/1-2-introduction-to-the-cathar-religion-2/

[48] *Cathar Church and Doctrine* article accessed on April 25, 2011 at http://lespiraldelconeixement.com/dossier.cfm?lang=en&id=42

[49] *Cathar Church and Doctrine* article accessed on April 25, 2011 at http://lespiraldelconeixement.com/dossier.cfm?id=44

The Gnostics had placed emphasis on spiritual knowledge (gnosis) as compared to faith; a self-knowledge obtained through understanding, courtesy of an inner, mystical (or esoteric) and contemplative experience (whereby one acquires knowledge of, and acquaintance with, the divine), coupled with purified living (conscious living) in keeping with all life.

In keeping with the beliefs of the Cathars, they rejected the idea of the death and crucifixion of Jesus. Instead, they stressed the reality of *living love*, a legacy bequeathed to them.

Their symbol of importance became the dove, which represented then, as it does for us today, "the idea of *peace*, or more accurately, the more subtle concept of *grace*, that state of being born in God's love." [50]

The Cathars were unorthodox in another important respect.

---

[50] Bradley, Michael. (1988) *Holy Grail Across The Atlantic: The Secret History of Canadian Discovery and Exploration* (p. 86). Willowdale, ON: Hounslow Press.

They "repudiated the idea of priests as intermediaries between God and man. The Albigensians had no priests. Instead, [they] had religious, or spiritual, leaders. These were called *parfaits*, or in Latin, perfectus … which means perfected ones." [51] In a further departure from Roman practice, "the Cathar *perfects* could be both men and women. In fact, by 1200 AD, there were more women parfaits than men." [52]

It was known that women in southern France had "a higher legal status than in the rest of Europe. A number of women held fiefs at the time of the Albigensian Crusade, and there were even famous women military leaders like Esclarmonde de Foix, who controlled the last Cathar stronghold," [53] meaning Montségur. [54]

It was in 1209 AD that the Vatican called for a Crusade against the Cathar heretics of southern France; a crusade that

---

[51] Bradley, Michael. (1988) *Holy Grail Across The Atlantic: The Secret History of Canadian Discovery and Exploration* (p. 88). Willowdale, ON: Hounslow Press.
[52] Ibid.
[53] Ibid, p, 89.
[54] http://www.catharcastles.info/montsegur.php?key=montsegur

spanned the course of thirty-five years and was clearly one of the most savage religious wars in European history, finally culminating in the defeat of Montségur (the mountain top citadel), after a ten month siege, in March 1244.

The defenders of Montségur (at least 225 of them) were burned in the meadow at the base of the mountain on which the castle sat, an area that is still called *Le Champ des Crémants*, meaning the Field of the Burning Ones.

One of the most challenging tasks we face is to learn to become nonjudgmental.

As you learn to let things be, disentangling from both emotionally charged situations as well as from the collective intellectual mindset of laws, rules and dogma, you are able to experience your own freedom and resolution.

A most suitable follow-up to my previous comments in relation to the Cathars.

While one may never be able to forget the atrocities that have taken place, all in the guise of religion, it is important that we learn to extricate our emotions from the event(s) in question, primarily because we create with our emotions and we need to become cognizant of what we are creating.

Perhaps there was a connection, here, between what Yeshua meant in saying, *Forgive them, for they know not what they do* because when we are so far removed from our true selves, we know naught the full impact of what we do (and do not do) and what we say (and do not say) against others.

Do not try to restrict others by judging them, controlling them or blaming them, for this limits your understanding of them. By direct association, this behavior also serves to limit their understanding of themselves.

Another most difficult, but absolutely pertinent, aspect as related to nonjudgment. Clearly, then, this is the way to remembering the sacredness of all life.

Just as you have experienced yours, so, too, must you allow others the time and opportunity to experience their own freedom, their own resolution, moving forward as best they know how.

There are no clearer words than these.

Whenever you judge people or situations, you envelop them within your own belief system. In this way, you blind yourself to the truth about them, forgetting that they, too, are whole and divine.

It is important to take the time to ingest the last few paragraphs, a bit at a time, feeling and meditating on the strength and truth of these very words, for therein you shall have arrived at your own enlightened understanding.

Many have forgotten their divinity. In so doing, they believe themselves to be separate from God. Within this forgetting lies limited beliefs, opinions and judgments, none of which are functional in navigating your way through to the higher expression of the God within.

Clearly, we are our own *perceived* limitation, are we not?

It is apparent that each individual must become aware of their own limiting belief system(s) so that they are able to effect the necessary change(s) from within.

As you gain in universal awareness, you quickly come to the realization that your divinity is also theirs as well. When you respond to people with love and compassion, you readily move from conflict to harmony. Such is the very freedom sought by all.

This is the essential formula to dissolving the negativity that exists, both individually and collectively.

When you remember, embrace and share your divinity, you free others to walk their truth. You become accepting of their truth, for such is whom they are.

Acceptance leads to unity.

Acceptance leads to connectedness.

Acceptance leads to oneness.

So, too, must you remember that we are continually evolving and changing as per our own individual experience(s). This also adds to both the greater collective experience as well as the totality of God, which means, as well, that God is also continually evolving and changing.

This also takes us back to the opening statement, a melding of *God-man* and *man-God.*

How delightful to be here, as individuated aspects of the divine, experiencing for God/dess, in such as way so as to add to the totality of All That Is.

How could it be otherwise for this loving energy that is ongoing and forever?

Enough said.

In fact, God loves us so grandly that we have been allowed, through choice and free will, to create our vast illusions of perfection and imperfection, good and evil, positive and negative. God allows us to express as we choose, without judgment.

These, too, are extremely powerful words that merit further thoughtful introspection.

We create our lives through our own thought processes.

Everything you think, you will feel. Everything you feel, you will manifest. Everything you manifest serves to create the condition(s) of your life.

Every word you utter expresses some feeling within your souls. Every word you utter serves to create the conditions of your lives. This is a direct fusion of thought with emotion.

Once again we are back to the power of emotion, coupled with thought.

This becomes where we can choose to live our lives as we wish, embracing either positivity or negativity.

Everything created by you has first existed in thought, followed by feeling. Knowing that the thought, then, materializes into your external reality, it becomes important to become increasingly aware of what you're thinking.

Most people are *enslaved by their thoughts*, thereby *creating by default* (creation by way of an unconscious means).

It simply does not occur to them that they can free themselves from the chatter of the mind.

There can be no peace of mind, no stillness, when one is engulfed by negativity, and, yet, inner peace is within reach of each and every individual.

Therein lies the juxtaposition, if you will.

When the mind is silent, happiness reigns inside and out. It is to one's advantage, therefore, to be able to still the incessant and compulsive chatter of the mind.

The majority are so deeply ingrained within the confines of the human race that they often defer their thinking to someone other than themselves.

Everyday life, for the multitude, seems to be fraught with worry, tension, anxiety and fear.

Thoughts arise in the mind, then, that also serve to reflect these outer feelings.

In order to break free (so as to regain control of their own mind), one first has to become aware of the problem.

Thereafter, one must work, consciously, toward reconfiguring how one thinks, how one responds, how one acts.

The source of all thought is, of course, the conscious mind; the segment that also deals with logic, reasoning (inductive, deductive, analytic and synthetic) and judgment.

The source of all power, on the other hand, is the subconscious mind; the segment that deals with intuition, emotion, inspiration, memory and imagination.

You must learn to think only about what you want, accepting it as part of your life. It is also imperative that you achieve vibrational harmony with what you are creating.

You will know that you have achieved, and/or are achieving, alignment with your thought(s) when you feel happy, contented, elated, peaceful, ecstatic, overjoyed, playful and upbeat.

The deeper the feeling(s) experienced, the closer the alignment.

Fearful thoughts create fearful situations and hard times. By direct association, when all of the citizens of this planet stop thinking about war and destruction, so, too, will these perils completely disappear.

We create by way of our emotional thinking.

Thought is the true giver of life that never dies, that can never be destroyed. All have used it to think themselves into life, for thought is your link to the mind of God.

Yeshua states this so completely, meaning that we are *always linked* to the mind of God/dess, and that the mind of God/dess is also to be found within our own.

Thought is the greatest force in the world; in truth, everything begins with thought.

Whatever you fix your thought(s) upon (meaning whatever you steadily fix your imagination on) is what you shall attract.

While all things are derived from thought, which is God, it is equally important to realize that God is not simply one formulated thought, but the reality of all thoughts.

Eureka … a light bulb moment as per Oprah, yes?

Individual truths, as held by you, as held by me, are all true, for each expresses the truth(s) of their experience at any given moment in time.

Change is an important constant. In keeping, our truth(s) change as our consciousness changes.

While there is truth in all things, so, too, is there refinement in all things. In fact, each moment serves to refine truth, which is why God is not a state of perfection, but rather a state of Becoming.

Yeshua puts this so simply, so matter of factly, that one cannot help but nod one's head in complete agreement.

You, alone, are your greatest teacher. You, alone, are your greatest friend. Cease looking outside of yourself, for the path you are to follow resides within.

Only you can know what is needed in your soul for your own soul fulfillment. Only you can be the giver of your own truth.

While this is a very difficult place to reach, it is attainable. The spiritual journey is a solitary one, meaning that the journey is different for each individual.

There is no right and wrong way to tackle this sojourn of exploration. To thine heart, you must be true.

When you come to understand that truth is, and can be, all things, then you are free, no longer enslaved to laws, rules, dogma or intellectual understanding.

To learn to Become multi-faceted in your truth means that you are not one truth, but all truths.

So, too, is this a difficult concept for a great many. It all comes back to the way of nonjudgment.

Demonstrating love through compassionate allowing means that you must love others enough to allow the range of their experience.

Likewise, this concept can be a difficult one to embrace. It is, however, *the way.*

As long as you look outside of yourself, you will never hear the voice that resides within, the giver of all truth and the creator of All That Is.

Become who and what you truly are by *listening to the God within you.*

Become who and what you truly are by both knowing and accepting that *God speaks through feelings*, for they will be your guide to truth, directing you onward toward your individual path of enlightenment.

Each individual is the true creator and controller of his life. The purpose of life is to be part of it. The key is to live life *consciously*. Likewise, we are to *live fully* and *with intent.*

To transcend the mind is comparable to watching your thoughts and feelings pass by, choosing which thought and/or feeling to entertain at any given moment.

While stilling the chatter of the mind can aid in mental and physical relaxation, what is even more important is recognizing and acknowledging that you are not your mind.

Transcending the dualistic mind is the battle of surrendering the bullying of the mind (ego-dominated existence) to mindfulness (awareness of one's thoughts, actions and motivations).

Mindfulness means *being aware of the moment* in which we are living.

Mindfulness is *meditation in action*, allowing life to unfold without the limitation of prejudgment.

Mindfulness means *being open to awareness* whilst becoming the *Infinite Possibilitarian* that author Norman Vincent Peale addresses.

Mindfulness pertains to *existing in a relaxed state of attentiveness*, one that involves both the inner world of thoughts and feelings, as well as the outer world of actions and perceptions.

Choosing at least one activity each day, to carry out in a mindful manner (giving it your full attention), helps considerably.

If you are chopping vegetables, take the time to absorb the colors, the textures, the smells, the motions, the tastes.

If you are exercising on a treadmill, take the time to feel your muscles moving as you walk, run, jog, speed up, slow down.

That having been said, one can learn to live the entirety of their day in mindful meditation.

While it is imperative that you become aware of what goes on in your mind when you are going about your daily life, it is important that you continue to step back, thereby maintaining the stance of an objective observer.

Freedom experienced on an inner level is the freedom that all seek, for it *is the real freedom.* This is what you begin to experience when you are able to still the mind.

A calm mind is a powerful mind.

Peace, contentment, happiness and bliss are to be found when one experiences this silence, this stillness, this sense of calm.

Inner peace enables one to feel grounded, to feel balanced. In these stressful times, this is what is needed by all.

Developing the inner ability to still the mind will take you a considerable distance towards both attaining and maintaining inner balance and peace of mind.

This is what living consciously is all about.

In choosing to have specific conditions in our lives, we must first *become* that which we want to experience more fully.

Become the peace that you seek. Become the compassion that you desire. Become the forgiveness that you seek. Become the love that you desire.

These words were also lived by Mahatma Ghandi, a master of non-violence and peaceful resistance, the first to apply such to the political field on a large scale.

Compassion is your birthright. Compassion is your truest nature. Compassion allows you to view from an equal standpoint. There is no judgment.

Are you willing to forgive those who have wronged you? Are you willing to see beyond hate towards those who oppress you? It is only in answering yes to these questions that you can choose to Become *more than* the circumstances.

In breaking the cycles of collective response, one becomes the higher choice.

The outer world is your mirror, always *reflecting yourself back to you.* This simply means that your outer world is a direct reflection of your inner world.

If you embrace and feel love, peace, unison and truth, vibrating such throughout the entirety of your being, you will experience people (places, things or events) who live and emulate the same.

If, on the other hand, all you experience in your outer world is disharmony, aggression, hate, separation and falsehood, you will experience people (places, things or events) who display and manifest the same.

It is possible to transcend situations in your outer world, all through the shifting of your inner terrain.

Living a new truth must first start with the individual. You must have the wisdom and the courage to embrace this new life, this new truth, as your reality. This reality must then be lived in a world that may not always support that truth. This has been the undertaking of my entire earthly mission.

Although the author is unknown, I was able to locate a most pertinent concluding message.

The good you find in others, is within you as well. The faults you find in others, are your faults as well. After all, to recognize something in your outer world, you must have a reference point in your inner world.

The world around you is a reflection, a mirror showing you the person you are. To change your world, simply change yourself.

See the best in others, and you will be at your best. Give to others, and you give to yourself. Love others, and you will be loved. Seek to understand, and you will be understood. Listen, and your voice will be heard. Teach, and you will learn.

The healing of this world will come about as a result of the healing of thoughts, feelings and emotions. By virtue of your service to yourself and others, so, too, do you serve the Creator. In this way, you Become the greatest gift that you can offer.

Your ability to express forgiveness, allowing others the outcome of *their* own experiences, without changing the nature of who you truly are, is the highest level of mastery to which you can attain. Therein lies the healing of all illusion, all separation, all duality.

These are clearly the ultimate goals associated with enlightenment.

Commissioned by Nick Bunick

Author of *In God's Truth*

Reprinted with permission.

Chapter 18

To further substantiate the words of Yeshua, while on maternity leave, Madeleine contented herself with working on the following mini thesis.

We will never become "the Master of the Moment so long as we continue to bear false witness against ourselves, and if there is a morsel of truth to be found in the ancient teachings, we will never be able to perceive it, much less accept it, unless we first, make certain, that fundamental changes occur in the way we live in the present tense. *We must be prepared to change the way we feel, think and act at this very moment*, today, and quite possibly in surprisingly drastic proportions." [55]

---

[55] Hearth, William. (2008) *Ormus: The Secret Alchemy of Mary Magdalene Revealed – Part A: Historical and Practical Applications of Essential Alchemical Science* (p. vii). Delaware, NJ: Ormus Publications and Booksellers LLC.

While the truths of today can set you free, such is entirely dependent upon both your ability to see, and accept, this truth.

Many would say that truth is relative, but I beg to differ. Truth never changes; what becomes relative, rather, is one's point of view.

Truth 1

God/dess does not engage in the commerce of souls, as in the unrestricted sale of indulgences affiliated with the early church (as began in the third century).

Truth 2

God/dess does not believe in anything that takes life away from another (through such proponents as war, acts of revenge and suicide). This also includes loss of freedom, "which results from wrongful thoughts and actions, or negligent inaction." [56]

---

[56] Hearth, William. (2008) *Ormus: The Secret Alchemy of Mary Magdalene Revealed – Part A: Historical and Practical Applications*

Truth 3

God/dess does not insist that we perform rituals and blindly follow specific rites (celebrations, practices) out of sheer superstition.

Truth 4

Eventually, all will find their way back to God/dess, therein contributing to the blissful freedom associated with the heart-mind-body-soul connection.

Truth 5

The enlightened individual "does not pray to trees or mountains, stars or invisible giants, nor to other men and women. One becomes the prayer. One's very essence is prayer."[57]

---

of Essential Alchemical Science (p. xxviii). Delaware, NJ: Ormus Publications and Booksellers LLC.
[57] Ibid.

While there is a Holy War to be fought, which is a deliberate play on words, for no war can ever be considered holy, it is a battle where we must "face the enemy within and make a friend of our enemy; thus neutralizing the beast [ego, selfishness, power, control] within, we turn lead into gold and we achieve liberation from illusion and dismantle the [false] programming." [58]

While the metaphysical transformation that results is not an allegorical one, much had, at one time, to be cloaked in this way.

Far from it, this metamorphosis (meaning a profound change in both character and circumstance) is a physical change; a change that affects the mental, emotional, spiritual and etheric (the unified field, the holographic universe, universal consciousness).

Gnosis is a word that means knowing.

---

[58] Hearth, William. (2008) *Ormus: The Secret Alchemy of Mary Magdalene Revealed – Part A: Historical and Practical Applications of Essential Alchemical Science* (p. xxix). Delaware, NJ: Ormus Publications and Booksellers LLC.

Your knowing will become your liberation.

This is a personal experience, a sacred experience, one that is unique to the individual.

When you come to realize who and what you really are, the sense of separation, long imposed, disappears, filling you, instead, with a sense of unity, a sense of connectedness, a sense of oneness with all that exists.

The peace of mind that reigns supreme enables you to concern yourself with the *living word* (the thoughts, words, actions and deeds that give life), while also demonstrating discernment because some will not be ready.

All, at some point, will make this innermost self-journey.

You are here to take the road less travelled, turning your eyes inward, for therein shall you locate what is needed.

Everything exists within.

By their fruits (ways, thoughts, attitudes, actions), *ye shall know them.*

It is an awakening of the heart that releases us from the 3C's (confuse, confound, control), thereby leading to healing.

There is much that you need to do so that you can begin to live your life to the fullest.

[1] Changing the way you think, feel and act, both about the world, as well as towards others, is essential.

[2] Accepting the totality of yourself, that which includes both light and dark aspects, is an important step towards self healing.

[3] Forgiveness of self is of extreme importance.

[4] Embracing positivity, as the way in which you wish to live and experience life, is paramount.

[5] You must learn to release all negativity from your life (as in TV, radio, internet, newspapers and magazines) so that you can learn to detach.

You need to stop watching TV shows that employ violence and negativity, replacing them, instead, with laughter and reassurance.

[6] Exemplifying nonjudgment and compassionate allowing for yourself, as well as others, is key.

[7] Replacing fear-based programmed beliefs with those that resonate with your own inner truth(s) becomes the prerequisite to inner change.

[8] Reconnecting with Mother Gaia, on a deeply dynamic, vital and intimate level, is what brings you back to the simple and inherent goodness of day-to-day living.

[9] Knowing, understanding and believing, that change is always for the better, becomes the very mindset that will allow you to embrace change.

[10] Accepting your divinity, your connection with God/dess, and knowing that you have never been separated from the Creator, is an important step towards Becoming who you really are.

[11] Acknowledging your oneness with God/dess and all Creation, while living this knowledge, is what shall bring about a heaven on earth atmosphere in your life.

As you begin to live by way of your own example, so, too, will this empower others to Become who they really are.

It must be remembered that life is all about …

[1] balancing your energies (meaning thoughts, feelings, emotions, words, responses, actions).

[2] Becoming who you have always been.

[3] exemplifying peace, love, honesty, truth, compassion, wisdom, wholeness, acceptance ... on a daily basis.

[4] acknowledging the perfect beings that you are.

[5] loving, and experiencing, life, in the now, to the fullest.

[6] eliminating separation, hatred, greed, envy, jealousy and pride from your energies (meaning thoughts, feelings, emotions, words, responses, actions).

[7] living from the heart as opposed to the head.

[8] taking ownership and responsibility for your energies (meaning thoughts, feelings, emotions, words, responses, actions).

[9] exonerating the other person because you are responsible for you; there is no one else to blame.

Trust, surrender, inner silence and peace are all to be found in the place of one's heart-centeredness.

This is the place that you need to retire to, on a daily basis, for this is the place that encompasses the very essence of who you really are.

A place of restoration and rejuvenation, this is your home away from home, your inner retreat space, so to speak.

You are not here to ridicule, torment, judge, gossip or slander.

You are not here to be ruled by fear, guilt, despair, unworthiness or failure.

You are not here to be consumed by feelings of inadequacy, hatred, dissention, unhappiness or denial of self.

You are not here to blindly follow the collective mindset, the governance of laws, rules and dogma, nor are you here to restrict another.

Engaging in any of these behaviors merely results in creating more of the same for yourself.

Instead, you are here …

[1] to expand in your knowingness.

[2] to meditate within for the answers of which you seek.

[3] to see that God/dess exists everywhere, within all things and within all beings.

[4] to embrace change as the sole constant in your life.

[5] to allow all to Be as they are.

[6] to Become who you truly are.

[7] to experience your own freedom and resolution.

[8] to embrace the higher vibration.

[9] to move from conflict to harmony.

[10] to choose without judgment.

[11] to demonstrate compassionate allowing.

[12] to be happy, joyful and filled with peace.

[13] to be love.

[14] to display gratitude and trust.

[15] to believe in yourself.

[16] to be patient and loving with yourself.

[17] to learn to become multi-faceted in your truth.

[18] to listen to the God/dess within.

[19] to live lives of unlimited joy.

As crystals and stones retain the structure of their original organic material, so, too, do you retain the structure of your divine essence, the DNA structure that you carry.

You, too, must come to that very realization.

We are the stewards of the Earth. So, too, do our bodies deserve the same consideration as our planetary environment.

In truth, our greatness lies in our collective harmony, brought forth through both an open heart and an unsullied mind.

You are here to remember that you are free; you are powerful; you are goodness; you are love.

You are also here to remember that you have value, that you have purpose.

It becomes in having experienced complete alignment with God/dess (the originating source energy for everything) that you realize that all is, indeed, well.

It is the awakening of the spiritual heart that leads one to a place of unity, wholeness and oneness.

Chapter 19

Two's company,

Three's a family.

We welcome with love …

Sophia Sinclair LeBlanc

Arrived: May 13, 2006

Weighed: 7 pounds 7 ounces

Measured: 22 inches

The proud new parents

Madeleine Sinclair

Michel dit Sophie LeBlanc

Chapter 20

We've found what makes

a house a home,

and these ingredients are key ...

lots of love, plenty of laughter,

and the presence of friends and family!

We hope you will stop by

our new house soon and often.

Sophia Sinclair LeBlanc

Madeleine Sinclair

Michel dit Sophie LeBlanc

Chapter 21

September 13, 2006

Saint Mary's University has sponsored yet another archaeological dig. Coordinated by Jackson Ferguson, chair of the newly struck Cobequid Archaeological Research Evaluation committee, aka CARE, the research begun in May, on a 10-acre property in Gaspereau, has proven fruitful. Remnants of an early Acadian dwelling, dating to about 1678, a pre-Deportation residence, was uncovered. Likewise, pottery pieces, glass shards and pewter plates were also among the findings. Excavation work will resume May 2007.

Chapter 22

The skull represents the higher mind. In order to attain the higher mind (as represented by spiritual awareness and enlightenment), one must release themselves from the lower mind (as ruled by ego).

It has been said that "crystal skulls are used to connect with other dimensions and act as communicators between the worlds." [59] So, too, has it been written that "the skulls always attract themselves to their rightful custodians and are said to travel through time to find their rightful human communicator." [60]

Madeleine had been told that she'd lived a past life as a Lemurian during the time of Atlantis and that she'd also worked with crystal skulls at that time.

---

[59] Banighen, Tyhson. (2007) *Further Adventures with Crystal Skulls* article accessed on July 25, 2011 at http://www.energydetective.ca/index.php?option=com_content&task=view&id=29&Itemid=55

[60] Ibid.

She was also told that she'd spent time going back and forth between the Hollow Earth and the Pleiades, readying the crystal skulls for when they would be found again. Could this be why she resonated so strongly with the special skull that Madame Pêche, aka Jacques de Molay, had given her?

Told that "crystal skulls choose their caretakers and are here to assist them with healings and to impart information from this and other times, spaces and dimensions," [61] Madeleine had spent significant time getting to know Inner Glow.

In companionable silence, he had imparted several messages of special importance that she was to share.

Number 1

Crystals are gifts from Mother Gaia. They are the energy masters from whom humans can learn much.

---

[61] Banighen, Tyhson. (2005) *Coconino: The Crystal Skull Mentor* article accessed on July 25, 2011 at http://www.energydetective.ca/index.php?option=com_content&task=view&id=30&Itemid=55

By centering yourselves, you become much more receptive to learning from us.

Using your quiet, open and inquisitive conscious mind, be not afraid to ask questions. Let us, your teachers, provide you with an answer.

These answers will first come in the form of pure energy. You will simply feel that which we have been able to share with you.

With increased practice, you may hear a voice inside you. Rest assured in the knowingess that this is a result of our shared connection.

Our aims are one of peace. Love is the energy which transforms all. We emanate with love from the heart of Gaia.

Peace is the environment. Love is the tool.

Love is the doing. Love is the acting. Love is the changing.

Love is what enables the necessary metamorphosis that must occur.

We are the old ones, the wise ones, the ancient ones. In a call to cosmic alignment, we are grateful to be here to assist you in your vision of transformation.

Number 2

Truly, there is no secret aside from the fact that such has remained hidden for millennia because the mystery teachings were forced underground.

Now is the time for them to be shared, openly and freely, with the citizens of this planet.

Number 3

Thinking that what you are looking for is to be found outside of yourselves, there have been too many questions put forth for far too long.

You have not yet dedicated enough time to learning how to delve within.

You must learn to quiet the mind, for it is there, and only there, that you will find what it is that you are looking for.

This is what Yeshua meant when he said, *Know what is in front of your face, and what is hidden from you will be disclosed to you.*

There is nothing hidden that will not be revealed.

Number 4

We were once powerful tools used for healing the Body, Mind and Spirit, within such cultures as those belonging to the Atlanteans, the Mayans and the Aztecs. So much so, in fact, that many indigenous cultures such as the Pueblo, the Navajos, the Cherokees and the Senecas, have stories that have been passed down, generation to generation.

Belief in the healing properties of crystals has a very long history, as the rituals of medicine men in ancient tribes can attest.

In much the same way that computers on the Internet are interconnected, sending and receiving information from around the world, so, too, are all of the crystal skulls on the planet interconnected via an *etheric energy network.*

Now that I have become activated, I can receive information from within this energy network.

Likewise, I can also project information outwards to any crystal skull that is linked in this same manner.

Number 5

As an ancient skull, I am also a portal to other dimensions, depending on the frequency of the receiver. All are here to open up to the ancient that exists within their very being. It is time to re-connect within.

It is time to come together in love, peace, compassion and nonjudgment, holding these vibrations deep within your heart.

It is time to live these vibrations. It is time to breathe these vibrations.

As you breathe in the breath of life, it is important to acknowledge the sacredness of your being.

With every in breath, feel your heart expanding.

With every out breath, release all that appears to stand in your way, known and unknown, whatever it may be.

As your heart expands, your mind grows calm.

Feel your body relax as you enter into a meditative state.

Number 6

Every human being is on a spiritual path. It is important to understand that fear can be transformed through the ability to maintain clarity, wholeness and love. Love is the biggest factor. Where love resides, there can be no room for fear.

Everyone on the spiritual path experiences expansion and growth that is unique to them.

Fears may resurface from time to time, but not so that one experiences the misery and desolation anew. It is from this position of expansion and growth, this newfound awareness, this newfound freedom, that one may work on clearing away the residue of their traumas, their fears, their anxieties, thereby purging the idea of hell from all levels of their being.

As you experience the release of the residue from your physical body, your emotional body, your mental body, your spiritual body, it is essential that you have compassion for yourself.

Number 7

Your conscious mind is fed through your subconscious. All of creation is sacred. You are divine beauty. Embrace the very sacredness of which you have always been.

Embrace God. Embrace Goddess.

Allow God. Allow Goddess.

Integrate both of these aspects of your very being.

Feel reclaimed, renewed, regenerated.

Feel the wholeness that resides within.

Feel the wholeness that has always resided within, just waiting for this opportune moment.

Feel your vibratory truth resonating inside the physical vehicle that you are.

Number 8

Let your divine self show you a new pathway. Surrender to the great majesty of love that flows through you. All is transformed through love.

Harmony, balance, wisdom and love shall become your heartfelt companions. It becomes in demonstrating this newfound awareness that you will have eliminated the constraints that serve only to keep one bound to the illusion; healing emanates from you on a vibrational level.

You are creating a dynamism of freedom that will become more and more potent as love transforms all. At this time of fear and degeneration, it will take those who desire to free themselves to become the healers, the teachers, the leaders.

Number 9

It is time to create anew, to create with excitement and inspiration. It is time to honor your goal of bringing this vast energy of love through to human consciousness.

It is time to reclaim your legacy of love. It is time to activate this reality. It is time to anchor these vibrations.

It is time to create a new story. It is time to remember who you are.

It is time to reclaim your power. It is time to reclaim the energy of your soul.

It is time to become the crystalline beings that you are. Such becomes your path of service.

Let freedom become your goal.

<u>Number 10</u>

Blessed are the meek, for they are the ones who shall inherit the earth.

In referencing these words, meek refers to the gentle, the courteous, the kind, the patient, the mild, the compassionate, the loving, for these very souls are the stewards of the earth.

Number 11

You live in a world of infinite possibilities. Unfortunately, however, your 3D minds struggle with the truth that you are limitless beings, unable to fathom that you are connected to a Source of infinite power and consciousness.

As you learn to let go of the limiting mind, you begin to experience what it means, as an awesome spiritual being, to have access to infinite possibilities.

In order to embrace who you really are, it becomes imperative that you throw off the yoke of repression, the yoke of separation, the yoke of illusion, for therein lies the illusion of separateness.

Limits exist only in the mind, so what does that tell you?

Number 12

Possessing both divine intelligence and freedom of will, you are forever expanding the infinite consciousness that you are.

You are the creator of your reality.

You are not here to be led astray.

Rather, it is our hope that you can awaken to the divine intelligence that you are.

The perceived limitations that find their way to you are but illusions to awaken you, for it becomes in welcoming and accepting them for the very lessons that they impart that you are able to embark on your journey of rediscovery.

<u>Number 13</u>

One must become mindful of the moment in which they are living.

Negative thoughts beget bondage. Positive thoughts beget liberation.

The battlefield of the mind is the internal war that plays out between dark (ego) and light (mindfulness).

This is a battle that everyone must conquer.

A calm mind is a powerful mind.

Number 14

Truth is always ongoing, evolving, being created every moment. Truth is created by every thought that you have.

There is also a paradox associated with truth.

When you come to understand that everything is true and yet nothing is true, that is when you shall be able to see that just as you perceive truth to be that which you determine it to be for you, so may all do the same.

In the moment that you no longer give credence to a truth, it is no longer real, for you have since moved onto a new truth.

Number 15

Remaining true to yourself, remaining true to your own truth(s), while also making use of discernment, is what constitutes your authenticity.

It must also be remembered that truth(s) are variable from person to person.

Should you come face to face with a truth that does not resonate with your own, simply agree to disagree, as goes one of your favorite sayings, and then move on.

Everyone is on their own authentic journey, at their own juncture, within their own development and perspective. This is to be respected.

You are not here to judge.

You are not here to condemn.

Instead, you are here to make choices that will strengthen and enhance your own individual growth.

Number 16

You are privileged to live in a world that has been infused with a vital, living, conscious, infinite, fluid (malleable) energy. As vital, living, conscious and infinite beings, capable of change, you, too, are this same energy.

Life experiences are created by beliefs, imaginations, and emotions, all of which work together as one system.

Emotions (energy in motion), however, are the links that exist between the body, mind and spirit; an affiliation that must now be forged anew.

It is imperative that you learn to analyze (in a detached way) and challenge your beliefs. It is as equally important that you detach yourself from the hardened belief systems that continue to generate superstition, bias, discrimination, bigotry, intolerance, chauvinism, prejudice, ignorance, irrationality and premature (and sometimes perverse) conclusions.

Learning to release yourself from these negative outcomes is what shall begin to transform your inner world.

As you work toward attaining the inner peace (emotional freedom) that is needed, you are achieving self-healing.

It is also imperative to remember that as individual consciousness grows, so, too, does this affect the collective consciousness in a positive way.

Anything that you do to enhance your life in the here and now, can only serve to also benefit the unified field to which we are all connected.

You are here to respect your individuated differences; you are here to embrace empathy and compassion; you are here to create connections (inclusiveness) and a sense of belonging.

Number 17

One of the most challenging tasks you face is to learn to become nonjudgmental.

As you learn to let things be, disentangling from both emotionally charged situations as well as from the collective intellectual mindset of laws, rules and dogma, you are able to experience your own freedom and resolution.

Do not try to restrict others by judging them, controlling them, or blaming them, for this limits your understanding of them.

By direct association, this behavior also serves to limit their understanding of themselves.

Just as you have experienced yours, so, too, must you allow others the time and opportunity to experience their own freedom, their own resolution, moving forward as best they can.

Whenever you judge people or situations, you envelop them within your own belief system.

In this way, you blind yourself to the truth about them, forgetting that they, too, are whole and divine.

When you respond to people with love and compassion, you readily move from conflict to harmony … the freedom sought by all.

Number 18

Compassion is who you are. The keys to compassion lie in your ability to embrace all experiences as part of the one, without judgment; the greatest challenge that all face as they move towards greater states of personal mastery (the return to your truest form).

Demonstrating love through compassionate allowing means that you must love others enough to allow the range of their experience.

Number 19

Mastery of compassion means redefining what your world means to you.

It is not about forcing change upon the world around you. You, and only you, choose how you respond.

As a being of compassion, you are offered the opportunity to transcend polarity while still living within the polarity.

This is what enables you to move forward with life, a life filled with freedom, resolution and peace.

Compassion means living in trust.

Compassion means living with joy.

Number 20

You are not here to focus on the suffering and the misery that exists within this illusion, thereby adding to both the negativity and gravity of the situation.

Instead, you are here to take enough interest in the game of life (or divine drama, if you prefer), playing the game consciously in order to achieve the overall purpose; that of enlightenment.

Number 21

Duality refers to physical separateness of opposite, yet related, modes of being: male and female, light and dark, night and day, yin and yang, hot and cold, past and future.

Polarity, on the other hand, refers to the essence of the underlying unity of these dualistic pairs, meaning that you cannot have one creative force without the other; that both are needed to maintain creative balance; that both are merely two extremes of the same thing.

As a result, you were gifted with the opportunity to view yourselves from a different perspective, all of which was deemed both necessary and important if you were to truly know, understand and master yourselves in all ways.

Likewise, you were offered the opportunity to *transcend polarity while still living within the polarity*, a decision that enables you to move forward with a life filled with freedom, resolution and peace.

Clearly, each has served to contribute to the expansion of planetary consciousness.

Number 22

Madeleine has been able to interpret many messages of great import, all of which have been shared with you, courtesy of this publication.

It is imperative to recognize that all of humanity is united by a common origin via the seen and unseen aspects of creation.

Embrace that which is the shared collective of love, peace, joy, happiness, for it is that, and that alone, which is the very truth that shall set you on the path to freedom and release, Becoming that which you seek in earnest.

Love is the very energy that is bringing about the pertinent, and much needed, changes.

Might love, then, be defined as the very galactic wave (the Intelligent Design of which, we, too, are a glorious part) that is commandeering you to the next level: one of peace, freedom, compassion, fraternity, purity, intelligence, creativity, liberation, transformation, harmony, love, acceptance, unlimited beauty, virtue, new life, respect, tolerance, sharing, gratitude and forgiveness?

Living a new truth must first start with the individual. You must have the wisdom and the courage to embrace this new life, this new truth, as your reality.

You are part of a much larger Galactic family than you have ever believed possible.

Concluding Message

Such concludes the story of Maman and Papa.

In the coming together of two hearts, linked in the proper manner, left breast (the feminine) against right breast (the masculine), the proper way to embrace, I was born with the very same birthmark, that of the same Templar cross, but situated between my shoulder blades.

In keeping with the otherworldy events of this story, I was conceived in late August 1755 and born on May 13, 2006, a birth date also shared, interestingly enough, with JD (once known as Jacques de Molay), my godfather.

The gold pieces left to my parents garnished more than enough monies to purchase thirty acres of south facing, cleared farmland, in Upper Granville.

It was here that they were able to build a solar energy heated home, complete with a permanent terra cotta and turquoise granite resin Chartres Cathedral style labyrinth (situated outdoors) as well as a greenhouse.

A second building, detached from the homestead, was used for seminars and workshops related to the message contained within the Aramaic codex.

There was a meditation room that contained two seven foot base copper pyramids, enabling the facilitation of one's entering into the alpha state of consciousness faster and easier, further enhanced with an extensive spiritual library.

Complete with a zafu cushion (buckwheat hull filled) that conformed to your body, the zafu cushion was placed atop a zabuton cushion, which, in turn, provided cushioning under the feet and knees.

There was also an alternative healing resource area (to which Maman combined Reiki with crystal healing) as well as an indoor (stone) medieval, 10 circuit style, labyrinth.

You could say that this building served to further accentuate the highlights of their mission.

Life is but a road that we are here to traverse, with many paths all leading back to the same destination.

Together, we have proven to be an extraordinary triad, doing our utmost to live our lives focusing on Yeshua's message of resurrection, his rebirth from an existing life, as shared within A Travel in Time to Grand Pré, the prequel to this book.

Infinite Blessings, as Maman would say, *to all who have lived these pages with us*.

The Grand Pré National Historic site commemorates the area as an Acadian settlement from 1682 to 1755.

It was this area around Minas Basin that some 2,200 Acadian men, women and children were deported from Les Mines, almost one third of the nearly 6,000 Acadians deported from Acadie in 1755, with the deportation lasting into 1762. [62]

The "chief founder of Minas was a rich inhabitant of Port Royal, Pierre Terriau, who probably settled on Habitant River about 1675. Associated with him were Claude and Antoine Landry, and René LeBlanc." [63]

---

[62] Parks Canada. (2008). Grand Pré National Historic Site of Canada. *Putting Down Roots* accessed on December 22, 2008 at http://www.pc.gc.ca/lhn-nhs/ns/grandpre/natcul/natcul3_e.asp

[63] Herbin, John Frederic. (1991). *The History of Grade-Pré: The Home of Longfellow's "Evangeline"* (p 27). Bowie, MD: Heritage Books, Inc.

Others soon followed, including Pierre Melanson and his wife Marguerite Mius d'Entremont; hence, a vibrant community was to flourish along the rivers and shores of the Minas Basin.

By the "beginning of the 18th century, the area of Les Mines was the largest population centre in Acadie. In 1750, an estimated 2,450 Acadians were living there, with another 2,500 in the Pisiquid and Cobequid areas, which had originally been considered part of Les Mines." [64]

The village of Grand Pré "extended two and one-half kilometres along the uplands and consisted of houses, farm buildings, storehouses, windmills and the parish church of Saint-Charles-des-Mines." [65]

There are several reasons why Grand Pré has been so strongly identified with the deportation of the Acadian people; namely, [1] the detailed journal kept by John

---

[64] Parks Canada. (2008). Grand Pré National Historic Site of Canada. *Putting Down Roots* accessed on December 22, 2008 at http://www.pc.gc.ca/lhn-nhs/ns/grandpre/natcul/natcul3_e.asp
[65] Ibid.

Winslow in 1755, and [2] the fact that the area was chosen by Henry Wadsworth Longfellow as the setting for his epic poem *Evangeline: A Tale of Acadia*.

More than a fictitious character, "Evangeline symbolizes the perseverance of the Acadian people." [66]

It was John Frederic Herbin, local businessman, descendant of this exiled people, and author of *The History of Grand-Pré: The Home of Longfellow's "Evangeline"*, who purchased the site of the church and the cemetery of Saint-Charles-des-Mines in 1907, thereby establishing Grand Pré Park as a memorial to the Acadian people.

Interestingly enough, it was also Herbin who had done some excavating on the site near a stone-lined well situated near the French willows, uncovering foundations to a large building.

---

[66] Parks Canada. (2008). Grand Pré National Historic Site of Canada. *Grand Pré's Legacy* accessed on December 22, 2008 at http://www.pc.gc.ca/lhn-nhs/ns/grandpre/natcul/natcul6_e.asp

He believed this building to be the remains of the church itself. Taking some stones from this ruin, he erected a stone cross to mark the cemetery two years later. [67] Digs carried out by Parks Canada, in 1982, proved that he was correct.

Unfortunately this local businessman was unable to raise additional funds to further develop the site, so he sold the park to the Dominion Atlantic Railway in 1917, on the condition that the church site would be deeded to the Acadian people. [68]

With the railway assuming responsibility for the park, the grounds were landscaped in 1917.

Courtesy of the popularity evoked by Henry Wadsworth Longfellow and his epic poem *Evangeline: A Tale of Acadia*, hundreds of tourists began to visit Grand Pré by train.

---

[67] Parks Canada. (2008). Grand Pré National Historic Site of Canada. *Grand Pré's Legacy* accessed on December 22, 2008 at http://www.pc.gc.ca/lhn-nhs/ns/grandpre/natcul/natcul6_e.asp

[68] Ibid.

In 1920, the company unveiled the statue of Evangeline near the park entrance, close to the train station. [69] This bronze statue had been sculpted by Louis Philippe and Henri Hébert.

As a result of funds donated by Acadians all across North America, the present day Memorial Church was built, on the very ruins that Herbin had identified as belonging to the parish church of Saint-Charles-des-Mines, in 1922, by the Société mutuelle de l'Assumption, with the interior being completed in 1930.

The Government of Canada acquired Grand Pré Memorial Park in 1957, declaring it a national historic site in 1961.

The cultural landscape of Grand Pré, which also includes the Grand Pré National Historic Site and its surroundings, is currently on Canada's tentative list as a candidate for UNESCO's World Heritage list, "a list that denotes

---

[69] Parks Canada. (2008). Grand Pré National Historic Site of Canada. *Grand Pré's Legacy* accessed on December 22, 2008 at http://www.pc.gc.ca/lhn-nhs/ns/grandpre/natcul/natcul6_e.asp

properties of outstanding natural and cultural importance that are a part of the common heritage of humanity." [70]

In a November 15, 2011 article, *2.5 Million Fund for Grand Pré*, written for The Chronicle Herald, the province of Nova Scotia will establish a $2.5 Million trust fund to help manage Grand Pré as an UNESCO World Heritage Site if a nomination bid for the international designation is successful. [71]

---

[70] Nomination Grand Pré accessed on December 22, 2008 at http://www.nominationgrandpre.ca/index.html

[71] http://thechronicleherald.ca/novascotia/33106-25-million-fund-grand-pre

Appendix A

Orgonite appears to manifest curious instances of synchronicity, and has a less than subtle way of showing how it works (making it very obvious). It has the ability to change, almost instantly, the atmosphere in work places as well as situations where there are high amounts of stress.

It is also able to transform electro smog, sick house syndrome, unwanted and invasive energies from pylons, communication towers, Tetra and Microwave, and any other unwanted negative energies.

In short, this simple and subtle technology is improving the energetic quality of our environment.

Here are some quick facts about orgonite.

[1] Easy to make and works continuously.

[2] Turns negative energy into positive energy.

[3] Purifies the atmosphere, detoxifies water, ends drought.

[4] Eliminates smog and helps get rid of chemtrails.

[5] Helps plants grow better, requiring less water and repelling pests.

[6] Mitigates the harmful effects of EMF radiation from cell phone towers, power lines, computers, microwave ovens, etc.

[7] Disarms and repels predatory forms of life.

[8] Inspires a pleasant demeanor and balanced, happier moods.

[9] Frequently remedies insomnia and chronic nightmares.

[10] Helps awaken one to their innate psychic senses.

Chi Generator® [72]

Etheric Warriors Forum [73]

Multi Purpose Orgone Disk [74]

Operation Paradise by Georg Ritschi [75]

Orgoknight (UK) [76]

Orgon 2010 (a site in French) [77]

Orgone Australia [78]

Orgone Energy Balancing (US) [79]

---

[72] http://orgonetec.com/
[73] http://www.ethericwarriors.com/ip/viewtopic.php?p=4433
[74] http://orgonetachyondevices.loveomni.com/oronge%20tachyon%20multi%20purpose%20disc%20.html
[75] http://www.lulu.com/product/paperback/operation-paradise-%28standard-edition-bw%29/2705804
[76] http://www.orgoknight.com/
[77] http://orgon2012.over-blog.com/
[78] http://www.orgoneaustralia.com.au/
[79] http://www.orgoneenergybalancing.org/index.html

Orgone Products CT Busters (US) [80]

Orgone Pyramid and Crystal Harmonizer (US) [81]

Orgone (Tachyon) Pocket Devices [82]

Orgonise Africa [83]

Orgonite Information, Links and Resources [84]

Orgonite Moksha (UK) [85]

Orgonite, Radionics and Life Force Technology [86]

Québec Orgone (Canada) [87]

---

[80] http://www.ctbusters.com/cart/orgoneproducts-c-22.html

[81] http://www.worldwithoutparasites.com/Orgone_Pyramid_Crystal_Harmonizer.html

[82] http://orgonetachyondevices.loveomni.com/orogone%20tachyon%20pocket%20devices%20.html

[83] http://www.orgoniseafrica.com/

[84] http://www.orgonite.info/

[85] http://www.orgonitemoksha.co.uk/

[86] http://www.hscti.com/

[87] http://www.quebecorgone.com/catalog/index.php?language=en

Sea Orgonite (South East Asia) [88]

The Harmonic Protector (US) [89]

Ultimate Vision (US) [90]

Warrior Matrix Forum for Orgonite [91]

Whale Tactical and Practical Orgonite (UK) [92]

---

[88] http://www.seaorgonite.com/
[89] http://www.worldwithoutparasites.com/The_Harmonic_Protector.html
[90] http://ultimatevision.us/
[91] http://www.warriormatrix.com/
[92] http://www.whale.to/orgone/whaleorgone.htm

There have been a number of phenomena associated with crystal skulls: [1] individuals receiving healing, [2] psychic and intuitive individuals receiving messages, and [3] a powerful energy that can be measured within or around the skulls when activated.

There were originally thirteen life-size human skulls that "told the past history of this planet and the evolution of mankind" [93] as held by the Mayans of Mexico, the Aztecs of Mexico, the Pueblo and Navajos of south western United States, the Cherokee, and the Seneca of north western United States.

The Seneca Legend describes how Atlantis "was destroyed due to an abuse of the powers of the quartz crystals. In the book, *Other Council Fires Were Here Before Ours* by Seneca Grandmother, elder Twylah Nitsch, she tells us that

---

[93] Maloti, Mvanah. *Crystal Skulls – History and Description* website retrieved on May 24, 2009 at http://www.sangomahealer.com/skullsinfo.htm

Atlantis was originally part of the continent called *Turtle Island*." [94]

In addition, the Seneca Legend also states that "during the time of Turtle Island, all five races of the world occupied one great land mass. The white race, known as the Gaggans, occupied what was then Atlantis, in the northeast of the island." [95]

The Cherokee Legend says that "each of the twelve planets in the cosmos that are inhabited by human beings possess one of these skulls. The thirteenth skull is connected to each of these worlds. When joined together they formed a powerful electrical current." [96]

Why is it, however, that skulls are carved from crystal?

---

[94] Maloti, Mvanah. *Crystal Skulls – History and Description* website retrieved on May 24, 2009 at http://www.sangomahealer.com/skullsinfo.htm

[95] Ibid.

[96] Ibid.

If spirit inhabits all of matter, "crystals are the highest evolved conscious forms of the mineral or earth kingdom. In addition, crystals can be programmed to work with the human body's system of energy to amplify one's healing abilities or to expand one's psychic ability. Their crystalline structure is formed by perfectly replicating geometrical atomic lattice structures that are built up over vast periods of geological time." [97]

In keeping, "our computer age is based on quartz crystal technologies. Vast amounts of information can be stored and retrieved from within the lattices of a single wafer cut from one crystal. Natural quartz crystals are record keepers of the earth's evolution of consciousness, and because they neither change with age nor decay, they would be the best way to transmit vast repositories of information from one civilization to another." [98]

---

[97] Banighen, Tyhson. (2005) *Coconino: The Crystal Skull Mentor* article retrieved on May 24, 2009 at http://www.energydetective.ca/index.php?option=com_content&task=view&id=30&Itemid=55

[98] Ibid.

Perhaps crystal skulls are a means of both attuning with and accessing the collective consciousness. What is the collective consciousness? Some say that it means having access to the Akashic Records, belonging to both our planetary system as well as others.

But why carve crystal "into the shape of a skull? Is it because the skull is a symbol of death that makes us confront our own mortality? For some macabre reason, the skull shape does grab our attention. For that reason the skull was used on the pirate's jolly roger flag and by the Knights Templar and Masons in initiation rituals. In addition, shamans have used skulls to communicate with forces or consciousness on the other side." [99]

Ian Lungold shares that "as our consciousness increases, time seems to speed up. Time as we know it will cease to exist at the end of the fourth cycle, and in this eternal now of

---

[99] Banighen, Tyhson. (2005) *Coconino: The Crystal Skull Mentor* article retrieved on May 24, 2009 at http://www.energydetective.ca/index.php?option=com_content&task=view&id=30&Itemid=55

the fifth cycle each thought will bring instantaneous creation. If this is true even our illusions will be real." [100]

In continuation, Tyhson Banighen believes that "the message of the crystal skulls is that our consciousness needs to be as clear as a crystal skull or we will experience the horror of our misconstrued thoughts." [101]

It could well be that crystal skulls "contain the wisdom and the technology of transformation necessary for humans to become light beings. With the death of our personality, or our egos, we are left with our spiritual presence." [102]

It is known that crystals act as both acquisition as well as transmission devices; hence, the reasoning behind their serving as the main component for computerized instruments of all kinds.

---

[100] Banighen, Tyhson. (2005) *Coconino: The Crystal Skull Mentor* article retrieved on May 24, 2009 at http://www.energydetective.ca/index.php?option=com_content&task=view&id=30&Itemid=55
[101] Ibid.
[102] Ibid.

Individuals purchase crystals for a wide variety of reasons: their beauty, their air of mystery, their metaphysical properties, the messages that they have stored throughout their existence on this planet.

To the native peoples, crystals and stones are often referred to as *grandfathers*, a point which seems especially fitting. Within this last century, some of the oldest known crystals have manifested in the form of skulls. Spending time with crystal skulls allows one to enter a dream-like state in order to access information about the past. Likewise, so, too, can they direct our higher selves towards the magnificent future.

Quite simply, they are vehicles of information, complete with images that have been stored within their crystalline structure for countless ages. Like anything, however, such power can be used to control others and to aggrandize one's self.

In keeping with the mystery surrounding the thirteen crystal skulls, no doubt this is why they were separated.

It has been said that the skulls were a gift, to the people of this planet, from the star people, or extra-terrestrials, who came from the Pleiades, from Orion, from Sirius.

Furthermore, it has been shared that "these crystal skulls contained all the knowledge of these people from the other planets. The skulls contained all their culture, their math, their science, their astronomy and philosophy; it included their hopes and dreams. Everything that they were was stored in those skulls." [103] Mind you, these skulls also had another function. They were to be "the template for a new species." [104]

While many may scoff at such a thought, there is something long hinted at in Genesis 6:2, where it says that *the sons of Gods saw the daughters of men, and found them fair*.

---

[103] Morton, Chris and Thomas, Ceri Louise. *The Mystery of the Crystal Skulls* online excerpt accessed on August 20, 2009 at http://goldenagetoday.com/departments/golden-age-articles/43-articles-paranormal/117-the-mystery-of-the-crystal-skulls?tmpl=component&print=1&page=

[104] Ibid.

It has been further stated that these extra-terrestrials "spliced the genes of the Earth people together with their own in order to help both species survive, but in a new form different from either of those that had come before." [105] While many may find this hard to believe, let us not forget that we currently have the power to do likewise.

Is it, therefore, so far off as to concur that another species, our direct celestial ancestors, would have had the same knowledge?

This is why "there are Indigenous people all over the world, not only from the Americas, who talk of our origins in the stars and of the ancient sky gods. The Mayans, the Sioux, the Cherokee all say that they originated in the stars. There is a tribe in Africa, the Dogon, that has always maintained that their ancestors came from Sirius, which they said was a double star system. Nobody believed them until our

---

[105] Morton, Chris and Thomas, Ceri Louise. *The Mystery of the Crystal Skulls* online excerpt accessed on August 20, 2009 at http://goldenagetoday.com/departments/golden-age-articles/43-articles-paranormal/117-the-mystery-of-the-crystal-skulls?tmpl=component&print=1&page=

telescopes became powerful enough to detect that there were, in fact, two stars there." [106]

Does this not encourage one to open their minds further to the very possibility that these so-called legends, held by the Indigenous peoples are, in fact, true?

There are also others "who say we come from the Earth. Both are correct, for we each have two lines of ancestry and genetic memory." [107]

Might this be associated with the very fact that our DNA contains two strands?

In continuation, "one of the reasons why the skulls were made of quartz is because silicon was introduced into our genetic structure by the sky gods. We were entirely a carbon based life form, but silicon is now in our blood. So within us is a part of the whole crystalline matrix that can

---

[106] Morton, Chris and Thomas, Ceri Louise. *The Mystery of the Crystal Skulls* online excerpt accessed on August 20, 2009 at http://goldenagetoday.com/departments/golden-age-articles/43-articles-paranormal/117-the-mystery-of-the-crystal-skulls?tmpl=component&print=1&page=
[107] Ibid.

link us to the rest of the galaxy. Indigenous people have always known that the Earth, the sun and all the other planets, are linked by an enormous web of crystalline structure. The web is made of sound and colour. The whole universe has structure and order and is connected to this web, as is Mother Earth. This is why the crystal skulls draw people to them, because they trigger our inner knowledge, the knowledge that we are both carbon and silicon in structure. We look at the skull and we are reminded of the silicon structure that is within the fabric, within our very being, that links us to the rest of the universe." [108]

Jami Sams shares further in her continued disclosure. "My people say, 'Remember your source. Remember who you are and where you have come from.' And this is a message of peace for the whole of humanity. For the crystal skulls are there to show us our shared origins. For this is the heritage of all of the people of the Earth. We are all united

---

[108] Morton, Chris and Thomas, Ceri Louise. *The Mystery of the Crystal Skulls* online excerpt accessed on August 20, 2009 at http://goldenagetoday.com/departments/golden-age-articles/43-articles-paranormal/117-the-mystery-of-the-crystal-skulls?tmpl=component&print=1&page=

by this common background: black, white, red, yellow and brown."[109]

Whether one believes, or not, what has been shared here, is, in retrospect, irrelevant.

Whether the so-called experts, namely the scientists, the archaeologists, the anthropologists, can prove, or disprove, any of what has been shared is also irrelevant.

The importance, however, lies in one's connecting with the messages themselves.

---

[109] Morton, Chris and Thomas, Ceri Louise. *The Mystery of the Crystal Skulls* online excerpt accessed on August 20, 2009 at http://goldenagetoday.com/departments/golden-age-articles/43-articles-paranormal/117-the-mystery-of-the-crystal-skulls?tmpl=component&print=1&page=

The ever popular cult film, The Matrix, interestingly enough serves as a most suitable "allegory for our current planetary condition." [110] It has become quite evident to me, having watched this particular trilogy, [1] The Matrix, [2] The Matrix Reloaded, and [3] The Matrix Revolutions, that this particular collection raises "many questions about God, our group reality, our individual reality and our legacy: the biggest question being, *who is really in control and what, if anything, can we do about it*?" [111]

Long have we been conditioned to believe in a controlled concept of God. We have lived with various institutions telling us "how to live, breathe, think, pray, behave and conform to rigid and unnatural social mores and laws," [112]

---

[110] Abel, Dawn. (2003) *The Legacy of the Gods* (p 3) article accessed on August 20, 2009 at http://www.mayamysteryschool.net/pdf%20files/Director_Sept2003.pdf

[111] Ibid.

[112] Ibid.

all as a means of brainwashing us "with specific belief programs that limit our choices." [113]

From the control group side of things, we have been "targeted through technology and subtle energies to perceive and experience war, plague, poverty, death, destruction, fear and scarcity." [114] As a result, "the goal is for us to live in constant terror, under scarce survival conditions, which turn our waking environment into a living prison." [115]

People on this planet are now waking up from this long programmed sleep. They are waking up to the knowledge that they are responsible for themselves. They are beginning to realize that all receive their inspiration and direction from within.

Going back to the native communities, shamans have long known that "our dreams are the key to reality rather than the

---

[113] Abel, Dawn. (2003) *The Legacy of the Gods* (p 3) article accessed on August 20, 2009 at http://www.mayamysteryschool.net/pdf%20files/Director_Sept2003.pdf

[114] Ibid.

[115] Ibid.

other way around."[116] How is it that this can be so? It is so simple, really. You see, it is our dreams that "show us a side of life that we all live when our ego is no longer involved in the process of maintaining the physical. They show us what is *really* going on from an objective point of perspective, and they can also be prophetic, helping us to realize our own power as well as the very weaknesses that must be overcome to live unrestrained."[117]

Getting back to The Matrix, if you but take both your "current reality and your dreams, and transpose them so that your dreams are your reality and your reality the dream, you start to get the gist of the program."[118]

So, just who is controlling whom?

Is there any value to sending our children to war, to fight and to die? Where is the liberation in such an action? Such merely serves to keep us entrenched in a system that cares

---

[116] Abel, Dawn. (2003) *The Legacy of the Gods* (p 3) article accessed on August 20, 2009 at http://www.mayamysteryschool.net/pdf%20files/Director_Sept2003.pdf
[117] Ibid.
[118] Ibid, p 4.

little about our well-being. Is their pursuit of power at your expense worth it?

Clearly, The Matrix, then, is "a political machine, an economic machine, a social machine, a religious machine, a family machine, and any technology that programs and feeds off the people without them realizing it." [119]

That having been said, The Matrix raises "serious issues about choice, destiny, control and the nature of God." [120]

Each and every one of us can be deemed *the chosen one* if we can free ourselves from these unnecessary distractions (as that is all they truly are) in order to begin the search toward finding our own inner truth.

The key to "breaking through The Matrix prison is understanding that we each have a role in creating our own

---

[119] Abel, Dawn. (2003) *The Legacy of the Gods* (p 3) article accessed on August 20, 2009 at http://www.mayamysteryschool.net/pdf%20files/Director_Sept2003.pdf

[120] Ibid.

destiny if we follow our own spirit, our heart and our intuition, while refusing to play by other people's rules." [121]

We are the controllers of our own destiny. The Gods, as they have long been called, are, in retrospect, no greater than we are. Upon realizing that we can all become one with each other, that we have always been one, that we have never been separated from this oneness, such will lead to the creation of a new and unfettered consciousness, one that will permanently dismantle the programming of old.

To free yourself is so simple.

You must find the answers that reside within.

You are your own oracle.

You are your own guide.

You are your own inspiration.

---

[121] Abel, Dawn. (2003) *The Legacy of the Gods* (p 6) article accessed on August 20, 2009 at http://www.mayamysteryschool.net/pdf%20files/Director_Sept2003.pdf

Having been made in the image of the Gods, it can only be that we, too, are Gods ourselves, forever changing and Becoming.

It is time to take back what is, and has always been, rightfully ours.

Appendix D

During the initial reading, researching and writing phase of this sequel to *A Travel in Time to Grand Pré*, Michael Jackson made his transition to the spiritual plane on June 25, 2009.

Dubbed the KING OF POP, he was one of the most commercially successful entertainers of the twentieth century. With unique contributions to music and dance, along with a highly publicized personal life, such made him a prominent figure in popular culture for four decades.

Michael Jackson had a notable impact on music and culture throughout the world. Tremendously successful in breaking down racial barriers, he transformed the art of the music video.

With a distinctive musical sound and vocal style, combined with eclectic dance moves, he introduced us to modern pop music. Clearly, music was his love, his outlet, one that he shared with the world.

Being the humanitarian that he was, my favorite song, in recent years, has become *Man in the Mirror*, a ballad of confession and resolution, one of Michael's most highly acclaimed songs.

What follows below are the lyrics to this outstanding song.

I'm gonna make a change, for once in my life.

It's gonna feel real good, gonna make a difference, gonna make it right.

As I turn up the collar on my favorite winter coat, this wind is blowin' my mind.

I see the kids in the street, with not enough to eat; who am I to be blind, pretending not to see their needs?

A summer's disregard, a broken bottle top, and one man's soul.

They follow each other on the wind 'ya know, 'cause they got nowhere to go.

That’s why I want you to know.

I’m starting with the man in the mirror.

I’m asking him to change his ways, and no message could have been any clearer; if you wanna make the world a better place, take a look at yourself and then make a change.

I’ve been a victim of a selfish kind of love, it’s time that I realize.

That there are some with no home, not a nickel to loan; could it really be me, pretending that they’re not alone?

A willow deeply scarred, somebody’s broken heart, and a washed-out dream.

They follow the pattern of the wind, ‘ya see, ’cause they got no place to be.

That’s why I’m starting with me.

I’m starting with the man in the mirror.

I'm asking him to change his ways, and no message could have been any clearer; if you wanna make the world a better place, take a look at yourself and then make a change.

I'm starting with the man in the mirror.

I'm asking him to change his ways, and no message could have been any clearer; if you wanna make the world a better place, take a look at yourself and then make a change.

You gotta get it right, while you got the time, 'cause when you close your heart, you can't close your mind.

That man, that man, that man, that man; that man in the mirror.

I'm asking him to change his ways.

Better change, you know that man.

No message could have been any clearer; if you wanna make the world a better place, take a look at yourself and then make a change.

I'm gonna make a change.

It's gonna feel real good.

Come on!

Just lift yourself up.

You know you've got to stop it, yourself.

Make that change.

I've got to make that change, today.

You've got to; you've got to move.

Come on, come on.

You've got to … stand up.

Stand up.

Stand up.

Yeah, make that change.

Stand up and lift yourself, now.

Yeah, make that change.

Gonna make that change.

Come on, man in the mirror.

You know it, you know it, you know it.

You know … make that change. [122]

To me, the aforementioned words emulate the very words penned by Yeshua, words previously shared within the prequel, *A Travel in Time to Grand Pré*. Truly, if we cannot be honest with the person in the mirror, then we shall not be able to find honesty within our own lives.

The Grammy Awards 1988 version of Michael's *Man in the Mirror* video [123] is extremely powerful, especially if we are able to take something away from the combined message and video images; something that we can make our own, on a day by day basis, while living in the here and now.

---

[122] Lyrics courtesy of AZLyrics located at http://www.azlyrics.com/lyrics/michaeljackson/maninthemirror.html purely for educational purposes and personal use only

[123] https://www.youtube.com/watch?v=ljpl0neGk2Q

Despite the fact that Michael Jackson had become a commodity, a product to be sold, used and manipulated, what gives the moral nihilism of our culture the right to be able to delve, with a dark voyeurism, into the humiliation, pain, weakness and betrayal of another?

Clearly, compassion, competence, intelligence and solidarity are useless assets to possess, as did Michael, when human beings are slated as commodities.

There are many who would say that it is this pursuit of status, wealth and fame that can destroy our very souls.

Change begins within the very heart and soul of the individual.

To affect change in one's outer world, one has to first *make that change* within. Everything starts within.

Take the time to learn about who you are.

Do not let people tell you what you are not.

Never destroy yourself to help another for the simple, yet profound, reason that this hurts both individuals, meaning that you have to take the time to heal yourself while the other remains stuck within that particular creation.

Never be so presumptuous as to do something for the supposed good of humanity.

You know what is good for you. You know naught what is good for another. Instead, always do something that increases *your* vibratory level.

When each individual unit of humanity decides what they want, what increases their vibration, only then shall each realize that they have the capability within to build a new age of love, peace, joy, happiness, contentment, non-judgment, compassion and altruism.

As each works to increase their own level of vibration, such also works, in the same way, for that of the collective whole.

Let yourself be guided by the inner you.

Take the time to develop your own system of learning.

Take the time to develop your own philosophy, learning to become as wise as the serpent, and yet as harmless as the dove.

Like the vast universe that stretches out before us, one's mind, one's belief, one's body, one's soul, is forever evolving.

Change is the only constant that we need embrace, thereby allowing for continued expansion of the infinite potential that resides within each and every individual.

For Michael Jackson, the words in his songs were his thoughts. He cared deeply about humanity and the planet. He was bright, talented, observant, loving and giving.

For Michael, everything was for love, L-O-V-E.

He was passionate about his work.

He was the king of entertainers.

He was the king of imagination.

May you also delve deep to *make that change*.

Bibliography 1

This particular segment pertains to books that may be of interest to the reader.

ACADIANS

Arceneaux, Leon M. (2002) Beyond the Storm: An Acadian Odyssey

Arsenault, Georges. (2002) Acadian Legends, Folktales and Songs from Prince Edward Island

Aucoin, Réjean and Tremblay, Jean-Claude. (1999) The Magic Rug of Grand Pré

Barrett, Wayne. (1991) The Acadian Pictorial Cookbook

Bleakney, J. Sherman. (2004) Sods, Soil, and Spades: The Acadians at Grand Pré and Their Dykeland Legacy

Boudreau, Amy. (2002) The Story of the Acadians

Boudreau, Hélène. (2008) Acadian Star

Boudreau-Vaughan, Betty. (1997) I'll Buy You An Ox: An Acadian Daughter's Bittersweet Passage Into Womanhood

Clark, Andrew Hill. (1968) Acadia: The Geography of Early Nova Scotia to 1760

Cormier-Boudreau, Marielle and Gallant, Melvin. (1991) A Taste of Acadie

Donovan, Lois. (2007) Winds of L'Acadie

Doucet, Clive. (2000) Notes from Exile: On Being Acadian

Doucet, Clive. (2004) Lost and Found in Acadie

Doucet, Clive. (2005) Acadian Homecoming

Doughty, Arthur G. (2008) The Acadian Exiles: A Chronicle of the Land of Evangeline

Faragher, John Mack. (2005) A Great and Noble Scheme: The Tragic Story of the Expulsion of the French Acadians from Their American Homeland

Gerrior, William. (2003) Acadian Awakenings: Roots & Routes, International Links, an Acadian Family in Exile

Griffiths, Naomi. (2003) The Contexts of Acadian History, 1686-1784

Griffiths, Naomi. (2004) From Migrant to Acadian: A North American Border People, 1604-1735

Hope-Simpson, Lila. (2005) Fiddles and Spoons

Jobb, Dean W. (2005) The Acadians: A People's Story of Exile and Triumph

Johnston, John and Kerr, Wayne. (2004) Grand-Pré: Heart of Acadie

Laxer, James. (2007) The Acadians: In Search of a Homeland

Longfellow, Henry Wadsworth. (1995) Evangeline: A Tale of Acadie

Mahaffie, Charles. (2003) A Land of Discord Always: Acadia from Its Beginnings to the Expulsion of Its People, 1604-1755

Maillet, Antoine. (2004) Pélagie: The Return to Acadie

Parette, Henri-Dominique. (1998) Acadians

Roberts, Charles G. D. (1898) A Sister to Evangeline: Being the Story of Yvonne de Lamourie, and How She Went Into Exile with the Villagers of Grand Pré

Roberts, Charles G. D. (2003) The Forge in the Forest: An Acadian Romance (first published in 1896.

Ross, Sally and Deveau, Alphonse. (1995) The Acadians of Nova Scotia: Past and Present

Silver, Alfred. (2002) Three Hills Home

Stewart, Sharon. (2004) Dear Canada: Banished from Our Home: The Acadian Diary of Angélique Richard, Grand Pré, Acadie, 1755

Tallant, Robert and Boyd Dillon, Corinne. (2001) Evangeline and The Acadians

CATHARISM

Arnold, John. (2001) Inquisition and Power: Catharism and the Confessing Subject in Medieval Languedoc

Barber, Malcolm. (2000) The Cathars: Dualist Heretics in Languedoc in the High Middle Ages

Burnham, Sophy. (2002) The Treasure of Montségur: A Novel of the Cathars

Costen, Michael. (1997) The Cathars and The Albigensian Crusade

Cowper, Marcus and Dennis, Peter. (2006) Cathar Castles: Fortresses of the Albigensian Crusade 1209-1300

Craney, Glen. (2008) The Fire and the Light: A Novel of the Cathars and the Lost Teachings of Christ

Douzet, André. (2006) The Wandering of the Grail: The Cathars, the Search for the Grail, and the Discovery of Egyptian Relics in the French Pyrenees

Guirdham, Arthur. (2004) The Cathars & Reincarnation

Guirdham, Arthur. (2004) We Are One Another

Guirdham, Arthur. (2004) The Lake and The Castle

Hughes, Nita. (2003) Past Recall: When Love and Wisdom Transcend Time

Hughes, Nita. (2006) The Cathar Legacy

Lambert, Malcolm D. (1998) The Cathars

Markale, Jean. (2003) Montségur and The Mystery of the Cathars

Martin, Sean. (2004) The Cathars: The Most Successful Heresy of the Middle Ages

Mattingly, Alan. (2005) Walking in the Cathar Region: Cathar Castles of South West France

Moerland, Bram. (2009) The Cathars

O'Shea, Stephen (2001) The Perfect Heresy: The Revolutionary Life and Death of the Medieval Cathars

Stoyanov, Yuri. (2000) The Other God: Dualist Religions from Antiquity to the Cathar Heresy

Strayer, Joseph. (1992) The Albigensian Crusades

Vasilev, Georgi. (2007) Heresy and the English Reformation: Bogomil-Cathar Influence on Wycliffe, Langland, Tyndale and Milton

Weis, Rene. (2002) The Yellow Cross: The Story of the Last Cathar's Rebellion Against the Inquisition, 1290-1329

DNA STUDIES

Olson, Steve. (2003) Mapping Human History: Genes, Race, and Our Common Origins

Oppenheimer, Stephen. (2004) The Real Eve: Modern Man's Journey Out of Africa

Oppenheimer, Stephen. (2004) Out of Eden

Sykes, Bryan. (2001) The Seven Daughters of Eve

Sykes, Bryan. (2005) Adam's Curse: The Science That Reveals Our Genetic Destiny

Sykes, Bryan. (2006) Saxons, Vikings and Celts: The Genetic Roots of Britain and Ireland

Sykes, Bryan. (2007) Blood of the Isles: Exploring the Genetic Roots of our Tribal History

Wells, Spencer. (2004) The Journey of Man: A Genetic Odyssey

Wells, Spencer. (2007) Deep Ancestry: Inside the Genographic Project

HOLY BLOODLINE, HOLY GRAIL

Andrews, Richard. (1996) The Tomb of God: The Body of Jesus and The Solution To A 2,000 Year Old Mystery

Arimathea, Joseph of. (1999) The Book of The Holy Grail

Baigent, Michael; Leigh, Richard and Lincoln, Henry. (2004) Holy Blood, Holy Grail

Bradley, Michael. (1996) Holy Grail Across the Atlantic: The Secret History of Canadian Discovery and Exploration

Bradley, Michael. (1998) Grail Knights of North America: On the Trail of the Grail Legacy in Canada and the United States

Bradley, Michael. (2005) Swords at Sunset: Last Stand of North America's Grail Knights

Emerys, Chevalier. (2007) Revelation of the Holy Grail

Francke, Sylvia. (2007) The Tree of Life and The Holy Grail: Ancient and Modern Spiritual Paths and the Mystery of Rennes-le-Château

Gardiner, Philip and Osborn, Gary. (2006) The Serpent Grail: The Truth Behind the Holy Grail, the Philosopher's Stone and the Elixir of Life

Gardner, Laurence. (2000) Genesis of the Grail Kings: The Explosive Story of Genetic Cloning of and the Ancient Bloodline of Jesus

Gardner, Laurence. (2001) Bloodline of the Holy Grail: The Hidden Lineage of Jesus Revealed

Gardner, Laurence. (2006) The Magdalene Legacy: The Jesus and Mary Bloodline Conspiracy

Gardner, Laurence. (2008) The Grail Enigma: The Hidden Heirs of Jesus and Mary Magdalene

Johnson, Bettye. (2005) Secrets of the Magdalene Scrolls: The Forbidden Truth of the Life and Times of Mary Magdalene

Johnson, Bettye. (2007) Mary Magdalene, Her Story

Lincoln, Henry. (2004) The Holy Place: Sauniere and the Decoding of the Mystery of Rennes-le-Château

Miles, Rosalind. (2002) The Child of the Holy Grail

Ortenberg, Veronica. (2006) In Search of The Holy Grail

Phillips, Graham. (2001) The Marian Conspiracy: The Hidden Truth About the Holy Grail, The Real Father of Christ

Pinkham, Mark Amaru. (2004) Guardians of the Holy Grail: The Knights Templar, John the Baptist, and the Water of Life

Simmans, Graham. (2007) Jesus After The Crucifixion: From Jerusalem to Rennes-le-Château

Twyman, Tracy R. (2004) The Merovingian Mythos and the Mystery of Rennes-le-Château

Wallace-Murphy, Tim and Hopkins, Marilyn. (2000) Rosslyn: Guardian of the Secret of the Holy Grail

Wallace-Murphy, Tim; Simmons, Graham and Hopkins, Marilyn. (2000) Rex Deus: The True Mystery of Rennes-le-Château

Young, John K. (2003) Sacred Sites of the Knights Templar: Ancient Astronomers and Freemasons at Stonehenge, Rennes-le-Château and Santiago de Compostela

KNIGHTS TEMPLAR

Addison, Charles G. (1997) History of the Knights Templar

Barber, Malcolm. (1993) The Trial of the Templars

Bradley, Michael. (1996) Holy Grail Across the Atlantic: The Secret History of Canadian Discovery and Exploration

Bradley, Michael. (1998) Grail Knights of North America: On the Trail of the Grail Legacy in Canada and the United States

Bradley, Michael. (2005) Swords at Sunset: Last Stand of North America's Grail Knights

Bradley, Michael. (2008) The Secrets about the Freemasons

Butler, Alan and Dafoe, Stephen. (1999) The Knights Templar Revealed: The Secrets of the Cistercian Legacy

Butler, Alan and Dafoe, Stephen. (2006) The Warriors and the Bankers: A History of the Knights Templar from 1307 to the Present

Dafoe, Stephen. (2007) Nobly Born: An Illustrated History of The Knights Templar

Dafoe, Stephen. (2008) The Compass and the Cross: A History of the Masonic Knights Templar

Gardner, Laurence. (2007) The Shadow of Solomon: The Lost Secret of the Freemasons Revealed

Knight, Christopher and Lomas, Robert. (2001) The Hiram Key: Pharaohs, Freemasonry, and the Discovery of the Secret Scrolls of Jesus

Knight, Christopher and Lomas, Robert. (2001) Second Messiah: Templars, the Turin Shroud and the Great Secret of Freemasonry

Mann, William. (2004) The Knights Templar in the New World: How Henry Sinclair Brought the Grail to Acadia

Mann, William. (2006) The Templar Meridians: The Secret Mapping of the New World

Picknett, Lynn and Prince, Clive. (1998) The Templar Revelation: Secret Guardians of the True Identity of Christ

Picknett, Lynn and Prince, Clive. (2007) The Turin Shroud: How Da Vinci Fooled History

Pinkham, Mark Amaru. (2004) Guardians of the Holy Grail: The Knights Templar, John the Baptist, and the Water of Life

Read, Paul Piers. (1999) The Templars

Robinson, John J. (1991) Dungeon, Fire and Sword

Sora, Steven. (1999) The Lost Treasure of the Knights Templar: Solving the Oak Island Mystery

Sora, Steven. (2004) Lost Colony of the Templars: Verrazano's Secret Mission to America

Wallace-Murphy, Tim and Hopkins, Marilyn. (2007) Templars in America

Wallace-Murphy, Tim. (2008) The Knights of the Holy Grail: The Secret History of the Knights Templar

Young, John K. (2003) Sacred Sites of the Knights Templar: Ancient Astronomers and Freemasons at Stonehenge, Rennes-le-Château and Santiago de Compostela

MEROVINGIANS

Baird, Robert Bruce. (2008) Merovingians: Past and Present Masters

Gardner, Laurence. (2003) Realm of the Ring Lords: The Myth and Magic of the Grail Quest

Geary, Patrick J. (1994) Before France and Germany: The Creation and Transformation of the Merovingian World

Murray, Alexander Callander. (2000) From Roman to Merovingian Gaul: A Reader

Murray, Alexander Callander. (2005) Gregory of Tours: The Merovingians

Wallace-Hadrill, J. M. (1982) The Long-Haired Kings and Other Studies in Frankish History

Wood, I. (1995) The Merovingian Kingdoms, 450-751

METAPHYSICS AND SPIRITUALITY

Ambrose, Kala. (2007) 9 Life Altering Lessons: Secrets of the Mystery Schools Unveiled

Braden, Gregg. (1995) Awakening to Zero Point: The Collective Initiation

Braden, Gregg. (1997) Walking Between the Worlds: The Science of Compassion

Braden, Gregg. (2000) The Isaiah Effect: Decoding the Lost Science of Prayer and Prophecy

Braden, Gregg. (2000) Beyond Zero Point: The Journey to Compassion

Braden, Gregg, (2004) The God Code: The Secret of Our Past, The Promise of Our Future

Braden, Gregg. (2004) The Divine Name: Sounds of the God Code (audio book)

Braden, Gregg. (2005) The Lost Mode of Prayer (audio CD)

Braden, Gregg. (2005) Unleashing The Power of The God Code: The Mystery and Meaning of the Message in Our Cells (audio CD)

Braden, Gregg. (2005) An Ancient Magical Prayer: Insights from the Dead Sea Scrolls (audio book)

Braden, Gregg. (2005) Speaking the Lost Language of God: Awakening the Forgotten Wisdom of Prayer, Prophecy and the Dead Sea Scrolls (audio book)

Braden, Gregg. (2005) Awakening the Power of A Modern God: Unlock the Mystery and Healing of Your Spiritual DNA (audio book)

Braden, Gregg. (2006) Secrets of The Lost Mode of Prayer

Braden, Gregg. (2007) The Divine Matrix: Bridging Time, Space, Miracles and Belief

Bunick, Nick. (1998) In God's Truth

Chopra, Deepak. (1998) The Path to Love: Spiritual Strategies for Healing

Chopra, Deepak. (2005) Peace Is The Way: Bringing War and Violence to An End

Coelho, Paulo. (1998) The Alchemist

Coelho, Paulo. (2003) Warrior Of The Light

Crowley, Gary. (2006) From Here to Here: Turning Toward Enlightenment

Das, Lama Surys. (1998) Awakening the Buddha Within

Das, Lama Surys. (2000) Awakening to the Sacred: Creating a Spiritual Life From Scratch

Das, Lama Surys. (2001) Awakening the Buddhist Heart: Integrating Love, Meaning and Connection Into Every Part of Your Life

Das, Lama Surys. (2003) Living Kindness: The Buddha's Ten Guiding Principles for a Blessed Life

Das, Lama Surys. (2003) Letting Go of the Person You Used To Be: Lessons on Change, Loss and Spiritual Transformation

Doucette, Michele. (2010) A Travel in Time to Grand Pré (second edition)

Doucette, Michele. (2010) The Ultimate Enlightenment For 2012: All We Need Is Ourselves

Doucette, Michele. (2010) Turn Off The TV: Turn On Your Mind

Doucette, Michele. (2010) Veracity At Its Best

Doucette, Michele. (2011) Sleepers Awaken: The Time Is Now To Consciously Create Your Own Reality

Doucette, Michele. (2011) Healing the Planet and Ourselves: How To Raise Your Vibration

Doucette, Michele. (2011) You Are Everything: Everything Is You

Doucette, Michele. (2011) The Awakening of Humanity: A Foremost Necessity

Doucette, Michele. (2011) The Cosmos of The Soul: A Spiritual Biography

Doucette, Michele. (2011) Getting Out Of Our Own Way: Love Is The Only Answer

Dyer, Wayne. (1998) Manifest Your Destiny: The Nine Spiritual Principles For Getting Everything That You Want

Dyer, Wayne. (2002) Getting in the Gap: Making Conscious Contact with God Through Meditation (book and CD)

Ford. (2005) Becoming God

Ford, Debbie. (2010) The 21 Day Consciousness Cleanse: A Breakthrough Program for Connecting with Your Soul's Deepest Purpose

Freke, Timothy. (2005) Lucid Living

Freke, Timothy. (2009) How Long Is Now? A Journey to Enlightenment and Beyond

Freke, Timothy, and Gandy, Peter. (2001) The Jesus Mysteries: Was the Original Jesus a Pagan God?

Freke, Timothy, and Gandy, Peter. (2002) Jesus and The Lost Goddess: The Secret Teachings of the Original Christians

Freke, Timothy, and Gandy, Peter. (2006) The Laughing Jesus: Religious Lies and Gnostic Wisdom

Freke, Timothy, and Gandy, Peter. (2007) The Gospel of the Second Coming

Gawain, Shakti. (1993) Living In The Light: A Guide to Personal and Planetary Transformation

Gawain, Shakti. (1999) The Four Levels of Healing

Gawain, Shakti. (2000) The Path of Transformation: How Healing Ourselves Can Change The World

Gawain, Shakti. (2003) Reflections in The Light: Daily Thoughts and Affirmations

Hansard, Christopher. (2003) The Tibetan Art of Positive Thinking

Hicks, Esther and Hicks, Jerry. (2004) Ask and It Is Given: Learning to Manifest Your Desires

Hicks, Esther and Hicks, Jerry. (2005) The Amazing Power of Deliberate Intent: Living the Art of Allowing

Hicks, Esther and Hicks, Jerry. (2006) The Law of Attraction: The Basics of the Teachings of Abraham

Hicks, Esther and Hicks, Jerry. (2008) The Astonishing Power of Emotions: Let Your Feelings Be Your Guide

Hicks, Esther and Hicks, Jerry. (2009) The Vortex: Where The Law of Attraction Assembles all Cooperative Relationships

James, John. (2007) The Great Field: Soul At Play In The Conscious Universe

Judd, Isha. (2008) Why Walk When You Can Fly: Soar Beyond Your Fears and Love Yourself and Others Unconditionally

Katz, Jerry. (2007) One: Essential Writings on Nonduality

Koven, Jean-Claude. (2004) Going Deeper: How To Make Sense of Your Life When Your Life Makes No Sense

Kribbe, Pamela. (2008) The Jeshua Channelings: Christ Consciousness in a New Era

Lama, Dalai. (2004) The Wisdom of Forgiveness: Intimate Conversations and Journey

McTaggart, Lynne. (2003) The Field: The Quest For The Secret Force Of The Universe

McTaggart, Lynne. (2008) The Intention Experiment: Using Your Thoughts to Change Your Life and the World

McTaggart, Lynne. (2011) The Bond: Connecting Through the Space Between Us

Millman, Dan. (1990) Way of the Peaceful Warrior

Millman, Dan. (1991) Sacred Journey of the Peaceful Warrior

Millman, Dan. (1992) No Ordinary Moments: A Peaceful Warrior's Guide to Daily Life

Millman, Dan. (1995) The Life You Were Born To Live

Millman, Dan. (1999) Everyday Enlightenment

Moses, Jeffrey. (2002) Oneness: Great Principles Shared By All Religions

Nichols, L. Joseph (2000) The Soul As Healer: Lessons in Affirmation, Visualization and Inner Power

Peniel, Jon. (1998) The Lost Teachings of Atlantis: The Children of The Law of One

Peniel, Jon. (1999) The Golden Rule Workbook: A Manual for the New Millennium

Price, John Randolph. (1987) The Superbeings

Price, John Randolph. (1998) The Success Book

Quinn, Gary. (2003) Experience Your Greatness: Give Yourself Permission To Live (audio CD)

Radin, Dean I. (2006) Entangled Minds: Extrasensory Experiences in a Quantum Reality

Radin, Dean I. (2009) The Conscious Universe: The Scientific Truth of Psychic Phenomena

Redfield, James. (1995) The Celestine Prophecy

Redfield, James. (1997) The Celestine Vision: Living the New Spiritual Awareness

Redfield, James. (1998) The Tenth Insight

Redfield, James. (1999) The Secret of Shambhala

Renard, Gary. (2004) The Disappearance of the Universe

Renard, Gary. (2006) Your Immortal Reality: How To Break the Cycle of Birth and Death

Rennison, Susan Joy. (2008) Tuning the Diamonds: Electromagnetism and Spiritual Evolution

Ruiz, Don Miguel. (1997) The Four Agreements: A Practical Guide to Personal Freedom

Ruiz, Don Miguel. (1999) The Mastery of Love: A Practical Guide to The Art of Relationship

Ruiz, Don Miguel. (2000) The Four Agreements Companion Book

Ruiz, Don Miguel. (2004) The Voice of Knowledge: A Practical Guide to Inner Peace

Ruiz, Don Miguel. (2009) Fifth Agreement: A Practical Guide to Self-Mastery

Schuman, Helen. (1997) A Course in Miracles

Schwartz, Robert. (2009) Your Soul's Plan: Discovering the Real Meaning of the Life You Planned Before You Were Born

Sharma, Robin. (1997) The Monk Who Sold His Ferrari

Sharma, Robin. (2005) Big Ideas to Live Your Best Life: Discover Your Destiny

Shinn, Florence Scovel. (1989) The Wisdom of Florence Scovel Shinn

Shinn, Florence Scovel. (1991) The Game of Life Affirmation and Inspiration Cards: Positive Words For A Positive Life

Shinn, Florence Scovel. (2006) The Game of Life (book and CD)

Talbot, Michael. (1992) The Holographic Universe

Talbot, Michael. (1993) Mysticism and the New Physics

Tolle, Eckhart. (1999) The Power of Now: A Guide to Spiritual Enlightenment

Tolle, Eckhart. (2001) Practicing the Power of Now: Meditations, Exercises and Core Teachings for Living the Liberated Life

Tolle, Eckhart. (2001) The Realization of Being: A Guide to Experiencing Your True Identity (audio CD)

Tolle, Eckhart. (2003) Stillness Speaks

Tolle, Eckhart. (2003) Entering The Now (audio CD)

Tolle, Eckhart. (2005) A New Earth: Awakening to Your Life's Purpose

Twyman, James. (1998) Emissary of Peace: A Vision of Light

Twyman, James. (2000) The Secret of the Beloved Disciple

Twyman, James. (2000) Portrait of the Master

Twyman, James. (2000) Praying Peace: In Conversation with Gregg Braden and Doreen Virtue

Twyman, James. (2008) The Moses Code: The Most Powerful Manifestation Tool in the History of the World

Twyman, James. (2009) The Kabbalah Code: A True Adventure

Twyman, James. (2009) The Proof: A 40-Day Program for Embodying Oneness

Vanzant, Iyanla. (2000) Until Today

Virtue, Doreen. (1997) The Lightworker's Way

Virtue, Doreen. (2006) Divine Magic: The Seven Sacred Secrets of Manifestation (book and CD)

Walker, Ethan III. (2003) The Mystic Christ: The Light of Non-Duality and the Path of Love According to the Life and Teachings of Jesus

Walsch, Neale Donald. (1999) Abundance and Right Livelihood: Applications for Living

Walsch, Neale Donald. (2000) Bringers of The Light

Walsch, Neale Donald. (2002) The New Revelations: A Conversation with God

Walters, J. Donald. (2000) Awaken to Superconsciousness: How To Use Meditation for Inner Peace, Intuitive Guidance and Greater Awareness

Walters, J. Donald. (2000) Meditations to Awaken Superconsciousness: Guided Meditations on The Light (audio cassette)

Walters, J. Donald. (2003) Meditation for Starters (book and CD)

Walters, J. Donald. (2003) Metaphysical Meditations (audio CD)

Walters, J. Donald. (2003) Secrets of Bringing Peace On Earth

Weisenthal, Simon. (1998) The Sunflower: On the Possibilities and Limits of Forgiveness

Weiss, Brian. (2001) Messages From the Masters: Tapping Into The Power of Love

Weiss, Brian. (2002) Meditation: Achieving Inner Peace and Tranquility in Your Life (book and CD)

Williamson, Marianne. (1996) A Return To Love

Williamson, Marianne. (1997) Morning and Evening Meditations and Prayers

Williamson, Marianne. (2002) Everyday Grace: Having Hope, Finding Forgiveness and Making Miracles

Williamson, Marianne. (2003) Being In Light (audio CD set)

Wolf, Fred Alan. (1989). Taking the Quantum Leap: The New Physics for Nonscientists

Wolf, Fred Alan. (2000). Mind Into Matter: A New Alchemy of Science and Spirit

Wolf, Fred Alan. (2002). Matter Into Feeling: A New Alchemy of Science and Spirit

Wolf, Fred Alan. (2004). The Yoga of Time Travel: How the Mind Can Defeat Time

Wolf, Myke. (2010). Create from Being: Guide to Conscious Creation

Yogananda, Paramahansa. (1979) Metaphysical Meditations: Universal Prayers, Affirmations and Visualizations

Yogananda, Paramahansa. (2004) The Second Coming of Christ: The Resurrection of the Christ Within You

Zukav, Gary. (1998) The Seat of The Soul

Zukav, Gary. (2001) Thoughts from The Seat of The Soul: Meditations for Souls in Process

Zukav, Gary and Francis, Linda. (2001) The Heart of The Soul: Emotional Awareness

Zukav, Gary and Francis, Linda. (2003) The Mind of The Soul: Responsible Choice

Zukav, Gary and Francis, Linda. (2003) Self-Empowerment Journal: A Companion to The Mind of The Soul: Responsible Choice

Zukav, Gary. (2010) Spiritual Partnership: The Journey to Authentic Power

SPIRITUAL THRILLERS

Asensi, Matilde. (2006) The Last Cato

Berry, Steve. (2006) The Templar Legacy

Berry, Steve. (2009) The Charlemagne Pursuit

Brown, Dan. (2003) The Da Vinci Code

Brown, Dan. (2009) The Lost Symbol

Caldwell, Ian and Thomason, Dustin. (2004) The Rule of Four

Christopher, Paul. (2006) The Lucifer Gospel

Christopher, Paul. (2009) The Sword of the Templars (book 1 of trilogy)

Christopher, Paul. (2010) The Templar Cross (book 2 of trilogy)

Christopher, Paul. (2010) The Templar Throne (book 3 of trilogy)

Christopher, Paul. (2011) The Templar Conspiracy

Christopher, Paul. (2011) The Templar Legion

Doetsch, Richard. (2006) The Thieves of Heaven

Doetsch, Richard. (2010) The Thieves of Darkness

Hougan, Jim. (2006) The Magdalene Cipher

Khoury, Raymond. (2005) The Last Templar

Khoury, Raymond. (2007) The Sanctuary

Khoury, Raymond. (2010) The Templar Salvation

Malarkey, Tucker. (2006) Resurrection

Moss, Kate. (2007) Labyrinth

Navarro, Julia. (2004) The Brotherhood of the Holy Shroud

Navarro, Julia. (2008) The Bible of Clay

Ray, Tim. (2003) Starbrow: A Spiritual Adventure

Ray, Tim. (2004) Starwarrior: Starbrow's Spiritual Adventure Continues

Sierra, Javier. (2004) The Secret Supper

Sierra, Javier. (2007) The Lady in Blue

Young, Robyn. (2007) Brethren: An Epic Adventure of the Knight's Templar

Young, Robyn. (2008) Crusade

Young, Robyn. (2009) The Fall of the Templars

Bibliography 2

This particular segment pertains to websites that may be of interest to the reader.

Archived Toltec Audio Minutes [124]

Catherine Baillon to Charlemagne [125]

Catherine Baillon to Theodorus II Dukas Lascaris [126]

Grand Pré National Historic Site [127]

The Toltec Mystery School [128]

William Hearth [129]

---

[124] http://www.sherirosenthal.com/library/library.html
[125] http://www.habitant.org/baillon/figure2.htm
[126] http://www.habitant.org/baillon/lascaris.htm
[127] http://www.northeastarch.com/grand_pre.html
[128] http://toltecmysteryschool.com/
[129] http://www.williamhearth.org/

About the Author

Michele Doucette is webmistress of Portals of Spirit, a spirituality website whereby one will find links to [1] The Enlightened Scribe, [2] an ezine called Gateway To The Soul, [3] books of spiritual resonance as well as authors of metaphysical importance, [4] categories of interest from Angels to Zen, [5] up-to-date information as shared by a Quantum Healer, [6] affiliate programs and resources of personal significance, [7] healing resource advertisements and [8] spiritual news.

As a Level 2 Reiki Practitioner, she sends long distance Reiki to those who make the request, claiming only to be a facilitator of the Universal energy, meaning that it is up to the individual(s) in question to use these energies in order to heal themselves.

Having also acquired a Crystal Healing Practitioner diploma (Stonebridge College in the UK), she is guardian to many from the mineral kingdom.

She is the author of several spiritual/metaphysical works; namely, [1] *The Ultimate Enlightenment For 2012: All We Need Is Ourselves*, [2] *Turn Off The TV: Turn On Your Mind*, [3] *Veracity At Its Best*, [4] *The Collective: Essays on Reality* (a composition of essays in relation to the Matrix), [5] *Sleepers Awaken: The Time Is Now To Consciously Create Your Own Reality*, [6] *Healing the Planet and Ourselves: How To Raise Your Vibration*, [7] *You Are Everything: Everything Is You*, [8] *The Awakening of Humanity: A Foremost Necessity*, [9] *The Cosmos of The Soul: A Spiritual Biography* and [10] *Getting Out Of Our Own Way: Love Is The Only Answer*, all of which have been published through St. Clair Publications. In addition, she has written another volume that deals solely with crystals, aptly entitled *The Wisdom of Crystals*.

She is also the author of *A Travel in Time to Grand Pré*, a visionary metaphysical novel that historically ties the descendants of Yeshua (Jesus) to modern day Nova Scotia. As shared by a reviewer, *Veracity At Its Best* "constructs the context for the spiritual message" imparted in *A Travel in Time to Grand Pré*.

Against the backdrop of 1754 Acadie, it was the blending of French Acadian history with current DNA testing that contributed to the weaving of this alchemical tale of time travel, romance and intrigue.

From Henry Sinclair to the Merovingians, from the Cathari treasure at Montségur to the Knights Templar, this novel, together with the words of Yeshua as spoken at the height of his ministry, has the potential to inspire others; for it is herein that we learn how individuals can find their way, their truth(s), so as to live their lives to the fullest.

At present, she is working on a manuscript entitled *Living The Jedi Way*.

Made in the USA
San Bernardino, CA
28 July 2017